I did not serve in Vietnam.

Early Praise for
BREAKDOWN, RECOVERY, AND THE OUTDOORS

A Vietnam veteran from a middle-class, midwestern home, I thought the author was writing my biography. He brought me back to my family's dining room table and my childhood at our lake home. I couldn't turn the page fast enough to find other of my life experiences.

~ Steve Kufus, military intelligence, Vietnam War veteran, and successful attorney.

Chris Bremicker has a rare gift for bringing the reader into every experience. His writing surges with emotion and candid expressions from his soul. Readers feel like they are along for the ride as he describes the joys and challenges of life.

~ Lee Peterson Baker, a writer, fundraiser, and marketing communication consultant.

Breakdown, Recovery, and the Outdoors is a moving and inspiring story of courage and self-discovery. Following Mike's journey from his breakdown to his recovery, from being alone to finding wholeness, was an experience I won't soon forget. Bremicker's style is engaging and vivid, a joy to read. Highly recommended.

~ Jane Lo, a Chinese-Canadian writer, English teacher, and author of *All I Ever Wanted*

Chris Bremicker's *Breakdown, Recovery, and the Outdoors* is a raw and personal story of survival, resilience, and healing. He shares his character's experiences in Vietnam and the struggles that followed, painting a vivid picture of how war changes a person.

Despite his family's concerns, Chris enlisted and faced both physical and emotional battles. But his story isn't just about trauma—it's about strength. He doesn't let war or addiction define him. Instead, he finds healing through nature, writing, and human connection.

~ Susan Bayer

BREAKDOWN, RECOVERY, AND THE OUTDOORS

RUNNING WILD

RUNNING WILD PRESS

CHRISTOPHER G. BREMICKER

For Kim

My parents gave me a love of the outdoors and a way out of schizoaffective disorder the Vietnam War put me through. The outdoors healed me as much as the therapy and medication my doctors at the veterans' hospital ordered. Without God's earth, I stood a snowball's chance in Hell of making it. But I did make it with my fishing rod, shotgun, skis, and my girlfriend's sobriety (helping me with my own). Her newborn daughter helped, too.

CONTENTS

OUTDOORS

RAISED OUTDOORS, I REVELED in the sunshine, like my mother, who proclaimed it a glorious day when the sun poured down on her back as she lay on the dock of our cabin in northern Minnesota. As children, we could not get enough of the outdoors, rowing our grandfather's wooden boat around the lake, sunbathing on towels in our front yard, or running against the wind pulling a bedsheet across the lawn, my sister at the other end, laughing with glee. We roasted hotdogs and marshmallows in the chimney of a burned down cabin down the shore, spent the night in a tent of a blanket hung from a clothesline, ate watermelons, gushing with flavor, and spit out the seeds.

We water skied, our parents buying a fifty-gallon drum of gasoline for the family who owned the boat. We fished at night with neighbors down-shore, our cane poles dipping then plunging as walleyes hit our lines. A sparkling path of waves led to a crescent moon, glowing in the stars. We motored to a private island, deserted in the middle of the week, and swam, made Kool-Aid, and heated Sloppy Joe mix on a fire we built on the beach. Our mothers and their seven children hung over the sides of the boat. One mother owned the boat, our mother along to supervise.

We made a sailboat of our grandfather's rowboat, with a sail of canvas, a mast and boom of birchwood, and an oar in an oarlock on the stern for a tiller. We rowed to the center of the lake, turned the boat downwind, and raised the sail that pulled us laughing to shore two miles away. The sail filled, the boat reached, and the wake streamed behind us. We christened the sailboat Robert E. Leak.

JACKSON HOLE

I

I LOOKED IN THE REARVIEW mirror of my parents' 1962 Chevrolet station wagon as the Grand Teton Mountains receded into the sunset. I had raised hell in Jackson Hole, partied with a group of friends, downhill skied a mountain opened by the first tram in North America, and picked up a girl who ditched the fraternity boys she came with.

Then I decided to join the Army.

"What would you say if I enlisted?" I asked the others at the Denny's restaurant we pulled into for dinner on the way home.

"I'd say you were nuts!" Wetzel said. "No women. Bad food. Discipline. You'd go crazy." Known as Hustler Wetz, he routinely picked up women from their table to ours for a drink, hookup, and a ride back to their apartment, his success at this astounding.

"The Army?" Andy said. "What brought this on?" Although only 19, Andy looked old enough to be served alcohol in a bar. He lived on a pretentious street in St. Paul, put on aristocratic airs Alan hated, and liked college, hanging around fraternity houses without pledging.

"I'm fed up with school. Up to here." I drew my hand across my forehead. "Two more years of college?" I had made the dean's list three quarters in a row, had enjoyed life away from my parents, but felt ready for something new.

"You don't have to go into the service. You're a student. They can't touch you." Lou protested on campus against the war, demonstrated at rallies, and spent a lot of time justifying his continued enrollment to the Dean of Students. Lou's hair fell to his shoulders while the rest of us wore blow dried haircuts. "I spent five days in jail to keep you out of the war."

"You'd be a grunt," Alan said. "Carrying an M50 machine gun and one hundred rounds of ammunition over your shoulder." Alan, an auto body mechanic and the only one of us not in school, knew what working meant and what it fully entailed. He hated Andy's upper middle-class ways, snobbery, and affectation.

"What about your career?" Les studied business administration and wanted to make it to the top by the age of forty. His father, a successful businessman, knew each rung up the ladder. Les protected Andy from Alan—who hated Andy—and Rob—who only disliked him.

"What career? I want the Army to tell me what to do with my life." I had job-hopped from a ticket taker at a movie theater to a delivery man to a stocker in a grocery store. I told myself the big time would come sooner or later and to enjoy my age.

"I'm diabetic," Rob said. "I've got a medical deferment." Rob disliked Andy and mocked his mannerisms every chance he got. He hated phonies and made fun of them with his deadly sense of humor.

"I hate that war," Vicky said. "Sending young men to a jungle to get killed. For what?" Vicky was the girl who had decided to hang out with us instead of her fraternity friends. She had felt up Wetzel on the tram, humped Lou in our motel room, and made out with me in the snow on the mountainside, drinking red wine from my bota bag. She wore a white turtleneck and black stretch pants to show off her figure. We had offered her a ride home for the pleasure of her company. Free-spirited, she accepted.

"For nothing," Rob said. "You got that right." Rob lived on a middle-class, well-kept street, his father was an engineer for the railroad and admirer of Hubert Humphrey.

"To keep the Commies out," my brother, Jim, said. Engaged to be married, though his fiancé was not on this trip, he had a student deferment, which he clung to, not wanting the military to disrupt his life.

"Don't the Viet Cong use tricks to kill Americans?" Vicky asked. "What's a Bouncing Betty?" She learned about the war from watching Walter Kronkite.

"It's a hand grenade that springs in the air and explodes in your face," Les said. We knew these things from listening to stories of classmates back from the war.

"What's a punji stake?"

"A bamboo shoot sharpened to a point and dipped in shit," Les said. "The VC put them in pits American soldiers fall into." These guerilla tactics terrified us, even though we were hearing them secondhand in the safety of being back home. The idea of a punji stake used as a biological weapon and being able to pierce a soldier's boot petrified us.

"What a nasty war," Vicky said. "They can't just shoot you with a bullet? I don't want to see you killed, Mike. If you want to be a hero, so be it, but *why?*" It was kind of touching to hear Vicky voice a fear for my life. She seemed to want me to change my mind, though appeared to admire my courage. I appreciated her concern, but it solidified my intent to follow through with the idea. It was the type of female concern I could get used to.

Our server appeared and took our orders, hamburgers for everyone except me. I wanted a BLT. I felt special, the only one not going back to school and joining Alan in the money-making world out on my own.

"Anything else I can help you with?" the waitress asked.

"Say, Tiger," Andy said. "Can you bring me a jar of Grey Poupon mustard?"

"I'll see if I can find some." She smiled, ignored being called "Tiger," took the menus, and put our order slips in the rack above the cooks.

"Say, Tiger," Rob imitated Andy. *"Can you bring me a jar of Grey Poupon mustard?"* We were in hysterics.

"If I want Grey Poupon mustard on my hamburger, what's it to you, Rob?" Andy leaned forward in his chair, threatening Rob.

"Just a joke, Andy," Les said. "Just a joke."

"Screw you, Rob." Andy simmered down, his feathers ruffled, and settled back in his chair.

"*Tiger?* What are you? A zookeeper?" Rob leaned back into the potential argument.

"Lou is serious," Les said, defusing one discussion by returning to the other. "You can get killed going into the military. Your chances of going to Vietnam are excellent."

"I want combat," I said, glancing at Vicky. "I'm sick of dragging books to school, writing papers, and lying in the grass. It's pointless."

"I know a man who got hit in the groin by a Claymore mine," Rob said. "Blew his balls off." Silence followed this statement.

"Nothing to trifle with," Les said. Though not necessarily afraid of going to war, Les preferred to stay in school. He believed in serving the country, but not enough to volunteer to join the military.

"The Viet Cong don't respect human life," Jim said. "They attack in hordes. Their men—and women—are expendable."

The server appeared with our meals on a tray. "Hamburgers all around, and a BLT for the new recruit. This is Wyoming, kid," she said to me, "we support the war. And, personally, I like a man in uniform." She must have overheard our conversation.

I looked into her warm, suggestive eyes, knowing I could get used to the kind of attention my idea was getting.

"Maybe I should enlist," Les said, seeking the same kind of approval from the server.

"Nothing wrong with serving your country," she said, then shifted her attention back to serving the table. "I found a jar of

Grey Poupon mustard in a corner in the kitchen. We don't usually serve it, *Tiger*."

"Hog Heaven, Andy," Rob said.

"Grey Poupon is gourmet mustard," Andy said to Rob before thanking the server and reaching for the jar to spread the condiment liberally on his hamburger.

"You'd know," Alan said.

"Do you want to walk point?" Lou asked, as we began eating our meals. "Be first to make contact?"

I felt a certain reality come through with Lou's question. I swallowed and replied with false bravado, "I would do it for the other soldiers. Service is sacrifice." I sobered for the first time since my bravado started, hoping the fear hadn't made me appear fake or transparently uncertain.

The restaurant began to get busy. People filled booths and tables. Our server was the only employee on duty as she ran from the crowd to the kitchen. One family's baby screamed as the server said, "I'll be back when you have decided."

"What about an ambush?" my reality checker, Lou, asked. "These things happen. I don't think you are considering the full scope of what you are saying."

"You'd never come back," Vicky said. "Or you could lose a leg or an arm. Or your mind." Her admiration had suddenly shifted to a sense of loss hinging on my use of the word "sacrifice." "Aren't a lot of Vietnam veterans screwed up in the head?"

"I heard they are doing better than people think they are," Les said. A realist, Les avoided myths and wrong thinking.

"You're not thinking straight," Wetzel said. "One year in a jungle full of snipers, AK47s, and machetes. And you are not my image of a baby-killer."

"I've made up my mind." My bravado was being challenged and I reinforced it so it would return without any appearance of doubt. "It's time to leave home and see the world."

"You're thinking of the Navy," Rob said. "Vietnam is not the world."

We paid up, Andy got my bill since I was driving and it was my parents' car, and we left Denny's for the drive home in the night.

I was about to leave my friends, family, and girlfriends for a tour of a war I might not survive. But I wanted adventure, danger, and excitement, not schoolwork, my mother's cooking, and making my bed.

RECRUITING CENTER

MY SISTER DROVE HER MGB sports car with the top down and her friend in the passenger seat. I was in the jump seat. We were headed for the United States Army recruiting station.

"I'll take the bus home," I told her as she dropped me at the recruiting station on a busy thoroughfare in town. I wore a T-shirt to show off my physique, and my muscles bulged under the white fabric.

"You're crazy," her best friend said. "Everyone is staying in school, getting married, or running to Canada."

"The smart ones join the Reserves or National Guard," my sister said.

"They'll train me to keep from getting killed," I said.

"Yeah, like all the dead ones they've trained," my sister's best friend said.

"He's thought about this," my sister told her.

"To hell with school. I have to do something. Three years is not that long."

"I just love you, Mike," my sister admitted. "And no one wants anything bad to happen to you."

"I'm bulletproof." I was young and genuinely thought I was indestructible, turning away to go into the center.

"That's what you think. Be careful. Get a job where you don't get killed, like a cook." Skillfully, my sister downshifted the gears on the racecar, decelerated in the busy street, and pulled over. The engine responded to her maneuvers.

I turned around and smiled, "I want to be where the action is."

"Darryl Simpson came home crazy," my sister reminded me.

"Not all Vietnam veterans are crazy," I rebuked. "Most have their marbles."

I waved, turned away from them as my sister pulled back into traffic, opened the heavy glass door, and entered the office as a recruiter stood up to greet me.

"How are you, young man?"

"I'm fine, thank you," I said suddenly needing to choke back a little anxiety about what I was doing. The recruiter's uniform was pressed crisp and clean, and, I have to admit, it was a little daunting. I wished I had worn a button-down shirt.

"Are you ready to make a difference for the country and in your life?"

"Yes, sir."

"I'm not a 'sir,'" he replied, "You can call me Sergeant. Sergeant Morris. What's your name?"

"Mike Reynolds," I said, gaining my confidence back. "And I want to be an infantryman."

"Why don't you just wait to be drafted, Mike?" the recruiter asked.

"I'm wasting my time in school," I blurted out.

Sergeant Morris smiled. "If you volunteer, I can bring you in on a three-year enlistment, and you can choose any MOS you want."

"MOS?"

That's Military Occupational Specialty. What field you want to go in. Basically, in civilian terms, what job you want," he explained.

"I want the Infantry," I said.

"Not a bad choice. It's the backbone of the Army. Queen of Battle. And if you want to make rank fast, the Infantry is the way to go. Here," he said as he opened a drawer in his desk and pulled out a glossy catalog, "this will give you an overview of the job descriptions. The jobs are listed alphabetically, but if they were listed in terms of importance, Infantry would be first."

"Thank you," I said, taking the catalog from him.

"As an Infantry Soldier," he continued, "you'll serve in the field, working to defend our country against any threats on the ground. You'll capture, destroy, and deter enemy forces, assist in reconnaissance, and help mobilize troops and weaponry to support the mission as the ground combat force."

"I can do that."

I looked up from the catalog, nodding, and taking a chance to look around the office. An American flag stood in one corner of the office, next to the flag of the state of Minnesota. A poster on the wall showed a soldier holding a rifle across his chest that said, "Choice, not chance." Another poster showed a man in a helmet standing in the hatch of a tank. Another poster showed a soldier in fatigues holding a rifle and kneeling next to a German shepherd. Between the professionalism of the recruiter, the decor of the office, and my curiosity longing to join, I began to feel welcome in the recruiter's office. I shifted my attention back to what he was saying, convinced I was about to find a place for myself. The recruiter and I discussed physical fitness, and he remarked on my physique. Wearing the T-shirt paid off as he sounded genuinely impressed. I liked working out, doing sixty pushups and twelve pull ups daily. Not yet needing to shave, athletic, semi-famous in St. Paul as a skier, and dating the most popular girls, my life was too easy. Uncertain of my courage, backing down in a fight instead of standing my ground, I wanted to prove myself or discover if I had any balls at all.

I enlisted for a three-year hitch.

Twenty years old, it was my decision—I did not need parental consent.

II

At dinner, I announced to my family what I had done.

"You don't want to go to Vietnam," my mother said. My mother was powerful, and her mojo could withstand Uncle Sam's wishes, but was still a concerned mother.

"Let him make his own decisions, Anne," my father said.

"I don't think I could handle it if something happened. I don't want to be a Gold Star Mother. Even the loss of a leg. Your beautiful skiing legs, Mike."

"Mom, a lot of men go into the service and don't go to Vietnam," I said, covering up my inherent—albeit uninformed—desire to get to the war.

"You better not go. I could not withstand your loss, or even the chance of you dying." She had baked acorn squash with a pat of butter in the middle, her specialty, and we ate in the beauty of the dining room lit by the sun shining through the bay window. A glass chandelier sparkled over the table. My father had a drink with dinner, a Manhattan, his favorite. The bourbon and sweet vermouth glowed in the glass of ice cubes with a cherry on top. I could taste it from across the table.

"When I went to war, everyone wanted to go," he said. The war was popular, not like Vietnam. And FDR was a president we could get behind to fight the Germans and the Japanese. He wasn't like Lyndon Baines Johnson—Low Blow Johnson. Isn't that what your friends call him?"

"That's what they call him at Harvard." My best friend, Chad, was a gymnast who got into Harvard on an athletic scholarship. I had seen him recently and he had told me I was better off at the state school instead of an Ivy League university.

"The Army will get you in shape," my father reflected.

"I'm in shape now."

"I reveled in my conditioning. We swam ten miles for graduation." My father had been on an underwater demolition team in the Navy and his sense of indestructibility remained.

"I waited for you until you got out," my mother said. "Living with my parents, I worked at the Emporium, and wrote you letters."

"Dad, you never told us about letters from Mom."

"They're in a box in our bedroom closet. You'll never find them."

"You never told me you kept them," my mom said.

"My most prized possession."

"You better come back in one piece," my mother said to me.

"I'll send you some cookies," my sister said. "My brother, a soldier."

"They won't take me. I'm in school and married." My brother was on his second beer—still sober enough to be congenial and not question my decision.

My family gathered around me, knowing I needed their prayers, praise, and support, as I stepped into an adventure that could change my life forever. My grandfather had been a doughboy in WWI and earned the *Croix de Guerre* for bravery. My father had been in the Navy. I was stepping up to carry on that tradition of service.

After such an important dinner my mother didn't even demand that I do the dishes. She did them herself.

DELAYED ENLISTMENT

I SIGNED UP FOR THE Delayed Enlistment Program as an inactive reservist, where the Army gave me four months before I reported to the induction center. So, I hung around the house for a month, hunted ducks at my family's cabin in northern Minnesota for a month, and ski bummed in Sun Valley, Idaho, for two months. At home, I had spent hours at the downtown public library, reading works by The Lost Generation writers, not going to school, not seeing my friends, and my mother said, spending too much time alone. At the library, I haunted the stacks, reading dusty old books on dark shelves, withdrawing books no one read. I was interested in Gertrude Stein's exercises in repetition? A Hemingway buff, I discovered Gertrude Stein—Hemingway's mentor and the person who had coined The Lost Generation—and her exercises in repetition.

I also spent a lot of time in our kitchen talking to my mother.

"Do what you are told to do," she said. "Let the others be heroes." She asked me to peel back the wrapper to expose the seam on the container of Pillsbury Doughboy biscuits, hit it on the corner of the counter to pop the canister open, then place the biscuits individually on a cookie tray and put them in the oven.

"Uncle Jim flies B52s in Vietnam." We knew B52s bombed civilian targets as well as military targets, but did not talk about it.

"He went to school for it. The Air Force Academy." Uncle Jim held the rank of major in the Air Force.

"I want action, not paperwork."

"Don't say that. I hate this war. What did the Vietnamese do to us?" She mixed dinner of rice, celery, and hamburger into what we called hotdish. It was easy to make, and her children loved it.

"Ho Chi Min is a communist."

"So what? He's five thousand miles from here." She poured coffee from a percolator that gurgled as it brewed.

"The Domino Theory explains this war. If Vietnam falls, Southeast Asia falls."

"Do you really believe that? Who came up with that one? Dean Rusk? What makes him so smart?"

"I won't get killed. I'm too smart for Ho Chi Minh."

"Do your job. Pull KP and guard duty. I don't want you in harm's way." She put the hotdish in the oven and cleaned the counter.

"You know me, Mom. I pull my weight. Even when I'm scared." I set the table for five of us, placing the silverware on cloth napkins, and pouring milk for my sister, brother, and me. My father was not back from the office, so I did not pour a drink for him yet.

"I wish you weren't like that."

"Some men get assigned good duty, like Germany." I laid cookies at each plate setting.

"I hope so. Your mother hasn't got the strength to handle your loss." She hugged me and held me for a long time. She wiped a tear from her eye. "Just come home in one piece."

With nothing to do, I fed pigeons in the park. I came home early from downtown, watched TV, and killed time until my father came home from the office. When he got home early, he permitted me to drink with him before dinner.

I wasted my time in that do-nothing routine for a month.

Andy took me out on my twenty-first birthday, and I discovered bars with glasses hanging from a rack over the bar, men in business suits, women looking for men, and men looking for sex. I fell in love with that environment and devoted myself every night. I tasted the booze and heard the bar sing to me, with its laughter, clinking glasses, and happy talk, so I ate dinner with my family then made my way to clubs and cocktail lounges, loving the environment with lady bartenders, music from a rock and roll band, liquor, and inebriation, night after night.

"I need a drink," I called Andy at four thirty each afternoon.

"Buster's?" The bar where I first discovered alcohol.

"Buster's."

"Pick you up in half an hour."

We parked the car, walked along Hennepin Avenue, where the lifestyle of booze, cigarettes, and sex emanated from the doors of Gay Nineties, Moby Dick's, and Buster's. Andy and I sat at the bar next to any two women who looked available. If they were parked in front of gin and tonics garnished with lime, we, based on experience—"field research," we called it—knew we had more of a chance getting their sexual favors.

We were new to picking up women, nervous, but ready for new experiences—ready to learn. Too many times our conversations would go something like:

"Say, Tiger," Andy would routinely start. "Do you come here often?"

"Only at the end of the week."

"Where do you work?"

"West Publishing. We're secretaries."

"Can we buy you a drink?"

"We're just getting ready to leave."

"Would you rather dance?"

"We're going. Nice talking to you." The women would slide off their bar stools, walk across the dance floor, and out the door.

"That didn't last long. You must have said something wrong." I would raise my arms and imitate a machine gun firing into the sky. "Shot down out of the sky."

"Let's finish our drinks then head down the street."

The scene and interaction would follow the same pattern at Moby Dick's, but with a couple of differences. It was a younger crowd, and there was a pool table there, so in addition to striking out with women (this time closer to our age), we would lose ten dollars each to a pool shark. Sometimes, though, a pretty girl would move across the bar to sit next to me until she decided I was too unsure of myself to bother with. Another girl would join us and Andy talked to her.

"Do you come here often?" Andy had asked her, sitting next to her at the bar.

"I'm here every night."

"Nice place," Andy said—Moby Dick's the worst dive in town.

"I wouldn't say that. Do you want to buy me a drink?"

"Say, Tiger, we'd love to. What'll you have?"

"Scotch and water." Andy ordered the drink. The bartender made it and placed it on the bar in front of the girl.

"What's your name?"

"Bridgette."

"I'm Andy and this is Mike." I let Andy do the talking.

"Does he talk?"

"Yes," I said. "I talk. What do you want to talk about?"

"Anything. I know a lot of subjects."

"Do you want to go back to your place after we finish our drinks?"

"Sure."

"That was easy," Andy said.

It was easy—and rare.

I do remember Bridgette though. After going back to her apartment, we sat around her kitchen table, drinking beer, and I told Bridgette I was enlisting in the Army.

"When do you go?" she asked.

"In February. I'm hunting ducks and skiing first."

Later, we got dressed and Bridgette walked us to the door. We kissed her goodbye, thanked her, and I said I'd call her.

Andy and I laughed all the way home. Bridgette was the first sexual experience for either of us.

And I never saw her again.

DUCK HUNTING

THE NEXT MONTH, **I** hunted at our family's cabin, taking a bag of decoys to the pass between our lake and a pond and laying them out. I watched a flock of one hundred greenhead mallards spiral into my rig, but did not shoot because I didn't have a way of retrieving them. They were beautiful to watch as they descended in slow motion, landed in among my decoys, then took off, skittish.

I met a young man in the small town where our cabin was. He was a loner, unemployed, outdoorsman, but turned out to be a good hunter. I had met him at the gas station while I was fueling my Jeep.

"Where did you get this thing?" he asked.

"My father got it in trade for a banking deal with oil wells in Montana. He and his partners got six of them, loaded them on a car hauler and brought them back."

"What are you doing with it?"

"Hunting grouse, but I'm really trying to shoot ducks."

"I know how to get some ducks. The Boy River is loaded with them. But you need a boat."

"How about a canoe? I've got a canoe."

"That would work fine." So, he talked me into taking him in our canoe down the river to jump-shoot ducks.

We laid the canoe alongside the Jeep, drove upriver where we shot ducks as they flew up from the shoreline, retrieved them, and laid them on the fiberglass bottom of the canoe.

It was a great day.

My share of the ducks hung in the garage at the cabin until I cleaned them, placed them in our freezer, or cooked them. I used our electric duck plucking machine to remove the feathers, gutted the ducks, and rinsed them in the sink at the cabin.

On other days, I would dress warmly, take the open-aired Jeep down back roads, lower the windshield, and shoot grouse over the vehicle's hood. I baked the grouse, the most delicious game birds, with potatoes and fed myself—living off the land. I kept a fire in the fireplace, did the dishes, and ate well, cereal and milk for breakfast, a sandwich for lunch, and grouse for dinner. When I got lonely, I took the Jeep into town, drank coffee at a restaurant, and talked to the waitress, Sheila.

"How was the hunting today?" Sheila would ask.

"Good. We shot five ducks on the Boy River. I cooked one and put the others in the freezer."

"Is Joe a good guide?" Joe was the young man I hunted with, and everyone knew everyone in that small town.

"Yes, he's great. He knows every bend in the river. How is business this time of year?"

"Slow. You're my first customer tonight. People will start coming in around six o'clock."

"Would you like a duck I shot?"

"Yes, bring me a drake mallard."

"I'll bring one next time I come in."

She sat down at my table and ran her finger along the tablecloth. "Don't you get lonely up here all by yourself?"

"I make do. I'm so busy hunting or cooking for myself I lose track of time."

"I'm always around."

"Yes. What do you like to do when you are not working?"

"I have a son I take care of."

"Who's with him now?"

"My mother."

"How old is he?"

"Five. Too young to leave him alone."

"Yes. Where is his father?"

"Who knows? He doesn't pay child support, I'll tell you that."

She invited me over for a steak dinner. We stood behind her house, grilled the steaks in her Weber, and baked three potatoes in her oven. Her mother, with whom she lived, joined us. Sheila turned the steaks with prongs.

"You're not a bad type. Not like Sheila's husband. He was the worst. You tell him, Sheila."

"Mom hates him," she said.

"He was a deadbeat. A one-night stand would have been better."

"Mom, I'm not that bad."

"Why did you marry him? I told you a thousand times he was no good." Sheila's mother sat in a lawn chair, her red rimmed glasses and bright lipstick lighting up her face, and fingernails painted a bright orange. "The worst!"

"Mom, I loved him."

"I hope this man is better. A soldier. You can write him letters. You can see him when he's home on leave."

"I just met him."

"What are your intentions with my daughter? Love her and leave her, like her father did me?"

"My father is a Korean War veteran. He left us when I was ten years old. She never forgave him."

"They're all deadbeats."

"I'd like to write to you," Sheila said.

We looked at each other and smiled.

Sheila took the steaks off the grill on a platter and walked them into the house where she put them on the dining room table.

Her son, Johnny, was already seated, so we joined him, as Sheila placed the steaks and baked potatoes on our plates. She said grace, "Oh Lord, watch over Mike as he goes to war. Protect him from harm, bring him home in one piece, and may we be true to each other. Watch over my family, as my mother enters older age, and my son starts school. Bless this food as it nourishes us and may it bring strength to us, for each day of our lives. Your will, not ours, be done, Amen."

"Amen," we all said. We sat down to a steak dinner.

It was a friendly meal. I would have not complained if it had turned into something more as I felt like I could have gotten used to the homelife Sheila had. The waiting had taken on a sense of anxiety, and, honestly, I had moments of doubt about my choice to join the Army. The decision weighed on me that night at Sheila's house and any time I was in the cafe talking to her. It was best to be alone and stay focused on hunting and Boot Camp. When she asked me over for dinner again, I politely found excuses.

Our barn-red cabin had two bedrooms, one with a bunk bed, another with a queen-sized bed, and a porch with another bed. There was a living room with a braided rug, heated by the fireplace. The fireplace also heated, an adjoining dining room with a row of windows that looked over the woods. The kitchen opened onto the porch through a stained-glass window. Built in 1933 by my great-grandfather, the cabin was our family's spiritual core.

I was watching the news when the telephone rang.

"Mike?"

"Hi, Dad. What's going on?"

"Oh, your mother is worried about you."

"She's always worried about me."

"She wants to know if you are eating right."

"Please tell her I have grouse and a baked potato every night for dinner. I'm eating better than you are."

"I'll tell her. What do you do all day?"

"I'm hunting ducks and grouse."

"Are you with anyone?"

"No one. I'm here all alone."

Dan Rather came on the news and announced an escalation in the war. President Johnson addressed the nation with a "heavy heart."

"We want you to come home. It's not good for you to be alone, day after day."

"I'm getting along."

"You don't sound right to me. You sound disoriented."

"Really, Dad. I'm okay. If you want me home, I'll come home, but I am doing fine. Actually, enjoying the routine"

"You've been up there a month. When do you leave for Sun Valley?"

"When the snow flies."

The south shore glowed in the evening sun as the lawn glistened white from our first snowfall. The woods intermittent with snow lying mostly on the trees that had not yet shed their leaves. The floor of the forest held pockets of snow and the grass in the lawn pierced the surface of snow.

My plate of half-eaten grouse was placed on the coffee table. The fireplace crackled. The last sunlight poured through the porch, casting a glow on the kitchen. I really was comfortable.

"We'd be happier if you came home now."

"Okay." I tried to hide my disappointment. "I'll be home tomorrow. I'll leave in the morning."

"Thanks, Mike. We'd appreciate it."

"Dad, you know I'm twenty-one years old, right?"

"Mike, have you been drinking? You're slurring your words. What did I tell you about drinking alone?"

"You said it's unhealthy."

"I said it's peculiar."

"Okay, Dad. Okay. I've had a few. A lot of people drink alone."

"We'll see you tomorrow. No drinking and driving."

"I won't. Aren't you being a little hard on me? I'm about to go into the Army."

"I don't trust you. No drinking and driving."

"Sure, Dad."

I was entering the Army, still a boy, and my parents' son.

SUN VALLEY

SEVERAL OF US WORKED in room service. Dick Smith—Smithy—was the boss and he didn't take any guff from us less experienced "youngsters"—though he did take most of the tips. Smithy was older than us and, like many people who lived in the hospitality industry, finally died in it, but not before he became a friend of mine moving into my dorm room for a place to drink himself to death. He always placed a fifth of Canadian Club between his feet and sat on his bed, pouring a drink every fifteen minutes.

Once, he took a cart of ten iced teas to the Kennedy cabin in the middle of a snowstorm and walked in the door of room service, yelling, "Stiffed!" The Kennedys had not tipped him, and we all had a laugh.

Grace, our receptionist, a local who had known Hemingway, told us stories about Papa that really brought the legends of his adventures to life. She told the story of him sticking up for an underage man whose ID was carded at the Boiler Room, a bar for celebrities. That story ended up with blood everywhere and at least two men in the emergency room.

Steve was a pimple-faced, gangly kid, preoccupied with scanty, crotchless panties.

Dave from California spent too much time in the sun. Dick said his brain was fried by the sun, but I always thought it was from smoking too much marijuana. Perhaps it was a combination of the two. Dave's only virtue, again, according to Dick, was that he knew when the surf was up.

I worked two four-hour shifts, from five to nine in the morning and five to nine at night and skied the rest of the time.

Between work and skiing, I further developed a drinking problem, every night at the bar, drinking my fill. I sat silently, sipped on a Manhattan, and ordered several more. I talked to no one, did not try to make friends, and enjoyed the taste of liquor and its effect. Don't ask me what I thought about as I stared at the glass of bourbon and sweet vermouth and watched the fire blaze in the roomful of families, couples, and me—the only single person in the place. Outside the windows, paths were shoveled through the glowing snow piled ten feet high.

In between shifts one day, I took a chairlift ride with Penny, a young, copper-haired girl who could ski better than most, and for sure, better than me. We had taken a ski lesson from Corky Fowler, who made jumping off cliffs on skis a fad, and who had appeared on the back of Ski Magazine leaping into thin air. To his surprise, I kept up with him on a harrowing run down the face of the mountain.

Penny and I talked shyly at first, then warmed to each other. We were among the youngest of the employees and it was natural to be unsure of ourselves.

"Were you born in Sun Valley?" I asked, our skis clicking beneath us on the chairlift as we moved up the face of the mountain. Runs descended from the peak and aproned to the base, where buses waited to take skiers back to the lifts.

"Yes, Ketchum."

"Where did you go to school?"

"In Ketchum. Ketchum High."

"Did you go to college?"

"Not yet. I want to, but right now I can't afford it."

"Are you a ski racer?"

"I was on the ski team in high school."

"Do you want to take a run together?"

"No thanks. I'll stick with the others. You can join us. We have some good skiers."

"No thanks. I ski better alone."

"Maybe next time."

"Do you have a boyfriend?"

"My mother says I'm too young for a boyfriend."

"Just asked. Nothing meant by it."

"Do you have a girlfriend?"

"No, but I'm not too young for a girlfriend. Do you want to meet for a drink after I get off work?"

"I'm too young to drink. They'd get you for contributing to the delinquency of a minor."

"How do you know?"

"I've been asked out before. The bartenders check my ID."

Penny and I did not get along or were too timid to get things right, and we parted at the top of the mountain, as she returned to the lonely group of employees of which she was a part, and I skied off to ski by myself. We were ill at ease with each other, although we liked each other enough to try again.

That chance soon came.

Dick lined up a helicopter ride for me up the mountain. He got drunk with the helicopter pilot the night before at the Ram and the next day the chopper waited for me on its pad. I was the only passenger, or at least that was the initial plan.

As I placed my skis on the rack of the chopper, I saw Penny drop her skis into the rack of a bus. I called her, she turned, waved, and I asked the pilot if he could take Penny, too. He nodded, the prop blast was starting, and I waved to Penny to hurry and get onboard.

She grabbed her skis, ran to the chopper in her ski boots, and placed her skis and poles next to mine on the rack. We climbed inside the helicopter that began to *whop-whop* its rotors maniacally, and it lifted, whirling the snow beneath us. Penny looked at me, grabbed my arm, and we watched Sun Valley Village turn to toys far below.

"Mike! I'm so glad you asked me. Helicopter rides are so expensive." She hugged me and held me as the chopper hovered off the ground. "I've never done this before."

I put my arm around her, and she leaned against my chest.

The chopper kept rising, its power hauling us to the top of the mountain, and Penny and I watched skiers far below fall away in the distance. Higher, higher we climbed, the pilot pulling back on the stick, and soon we were above the top of the last chairlift, where no one skied, and where a weather ball measured changes in temperature. A herd of elk grazed below us, and higher we climbed, until we were at the pinnacle of the mountain and the chopper began to settle. The pilot took us down onto the snow, landed, and the rotors whopped. With the prop blast whipping our clothing, we climbed out, withdrew our skis, and waved goodbye. The pilot lifted the helicopter into the blue sky, turned it around, and descended the mountain.

Penny and I hugged each other and looked at the view. Baldy Mountain descended below us, we were above the tree line, and the tops of pine trees, covered with snow, dotted the field of snow our skis stood on.

"We're above the Sawtooth Mountain Range. Look at the lodge. It's so tiny," I said.

"Sun Valley looks like an electric train village," Penny remarked.

"This snow has never been skied. We're above that herd of elk."

"Let's ski the mountain nonstop."

"Can you handle it? I'm going to let them rip."

"I'll be right on your tail. You underestimate me. I've skied this mountain nonstop many times. Another thousand feet won't bother me."

"The air is so thin up here. It's hard to breathe."

I put my arm around her and kissed her.

"What was that for?" she asked.

"I love you."

"Let's ski. Stop that mushy stuff. Save it for later."

"As you wish, madam. Lead the way."

"This helicopter ride is once in a lifetime. Let's not ruin it."

"My apologies."

We slapped our skis onto the snow, clamped on our boots, slipped our gloves into our poles, and pushed off. Penny poled and herringboned her skis to get a good start. Like a racer out of a gate, she pushed with her poles and skis to accelerate through the fresh, deep snow.

"I'm right behind you!" I yelled.

The pine trees, half covered in snow, sped past us, we weaved around them, and slalomed our skis in the field of trees that would have cushioned us if we had wiped out. The snow, pristine and untracked, glistened, rebounding in the powdery stuff, and sparkled when our skis threw up a rooster tail of flakes. The field of trees fell away from us, as if it did not want us to catch up to it as we skied over the edge of the world.

Penny led the way, her powerful technique turning through the deep snow, weaving between the pine trees, buried deep in the snow, and disappearing ahead of me, until I caught up with her, seeing a glimpse of the white hat on top of her copper hair, her legs swaying below her hips, as she rocked through the powder snow. Far down we went, through the pine trees, then skiing onto the plateau of the weather ball and dropping over a ledge that took us onto the open face of the mountain but still far above the ski area where the paying customers skied. Penny arched her skis, carved them into a long, cutting curve that took her past the top of the lift, where skiers got off, and accelerated down the face of the mountain, her legs like shock absorbers, taking the bumps with the strength of pistons.

She kept skiing, I was behind her, driving my skis with hers, as we approached the Roundhouse, and went over a lip that took us into Rock Garden, so steep I edged hard, angulated, while Penny took it with long, driving turns, that took her below the Roundhouse, onto the last face of the mountain. We fell fast toward the buses, and I was right behind her now, as we came to the apron of the mountain and swept to a stop at the base, twenty yards from a bus, and the helicopter standing right where we had gotten on. We laughed and held each other, fell onto the snow, breathing hard, took off our skis, and dropped them into a rack on the bus.

"That was wonderful! I thought it would never end. The mountain kept going and going."

"I was right behind you until Rock Garden. You let that mountain have it. Carving your turns straight down that pitch I had to angulate on."

"I knew you'd have trouble on that part. I couldn't resist. I just had to let them run."

"You uncorked them!"

"That mountain was begging for it."

Back at my dormitory room, we tore off our clothes, got into bed, and I was happier than I had ever been in my life. It was her first time, she gripped me, wrapped her legs around me, and gasped with delight. Never slowing, never stopping, always closer, ever closer, we made love all afternoon.

"I'm not going to tell my mother," Penny said.

"She'll be able to tell by the look on your face. You have a boyfriend."

"Do you have to leave?"

"Yeah, I have a shift at five."

"No, I mean to the Army."

"That contract is signed," I lamented, then smiled, "Uncle Sam wants me."

"I want you, too."

"You can have me when I'm home from the Army."

"I don't want you to go to Vietnam."

We looked into each other's eyes and held each other. I kissed Penny, and we were one, like skiing, falling off the edge of the world.

I went to work at room service and never said a word.

Penny and I skied and ate in the employee dining hall together everyday until I left Sun Valley to go home before joining the Army.

<hr>

Three days after skiing at one of North America's most expensive ski areas, I was in a mess hall with a drill sergeant yelling, "Eat up and get out!"

BASIC TRAINING

MY PARENTS DROVE ME to the St. Andrews Hotel where I roomed with two young men from the Iron Range. Like me, they looked young for their age and possessed a devil-may-care attitude toward the military. We were Midwesterners—innocent, brave, and fun-loving, but, unlike me, they had enlisted in the Army's Buddy System, which guaranteed they stayed in the same basic training company. They supported each other, and I had no one. My sense of doubt began to rise again.

We flew to Ft. Campbell, Kentucky where we spent three days in a holding company picking up cigarette butts. I read *Time Magazine* and wore street clothes—my last contact with the civilian world. Then, on the fourth day, with a full duffel bag, and wearing brand new fatigues, a little sergeant with a clipboard ordered us to board a bus and shout, "Here, Sergeant!" as loudly as we could when he called our name. In a model of Army efficiency, we boarded the bus and rode over to our basic training company to become soldiers.

Over the next eight weeks, the drill sergeants taught us to do push-ups, march, run, do pull-ups, run again, do push-ups again, run again, march again, do pull-ups again, to run again, do push-ups again, and to kill people while avoiding being killed. And all of this was done while running around screaming, and yelling, "yes, Sergeant!" and "No, Sergeant!"

In Kentucky, at the time, there was an insane asylum in Danville. We were quickly convinced that Fort Campbell was an extension of that hospital.

As part of our training to kill people, we also practiced with the bayonet, the spirit of which was "to kill!" and we conveyed that spirit with enthusiasm by yelling, "kill!" on a heavy, rain-laden day on a parade field.

"What's the spirit of the bayonet?" a sergeant would ask.

"To kill, Drill Sergeant!" we yelled in return.

During one block of bayonet instruction, Drill Sergeant Lucas stood on a platform, drank codeine out of a bottle because he had a cold, and yelled, "You men are all fucked up!" He took a swig every minute or two.

Our company commander, a captain, stood to one side of our formation and watched. "Sergeant Lucas, that's the post commander's house across the street. His wife is home. She appreciates 'clean language,' so drive on to let her know what we appreciate."

We plunged our bayonets into thick rubber enemies. Our entire company lined up in a platoon and skewered, disemboweled, and eviscerated Charlie Cong in effigy.

My best friend in basic training, Ben Gillette, and I smiled at each other as we thrust the blades attached to our M14 rifles, and kicked, pulled back, ran to the next rubber dummy, and plunged again.

February in Kentucky, I expected flowers to bloom, sixty-degree temperatures, and no snow. The weather was frigid, we ran in cadence after a snowstorm, for three miles, our boots sopped in the one-foot snowfall. It got warmer in March, and during marches to the firing range there were a few days when we actually sweated in the sun.

We practiced close-quarter combat with pugil sticks. With padding at each end, the poles did no harm, but knocked men backward or off their feet. We jousted like medieval knights with lances. We battled each other in a contest until one man left standing.

Ben Gillette faced off with another man for the final joust.

"C'mon, Ben!" I yelled. "Knock him on his ass!" The jousting started. Ben lunged, parried, and blocked.

"Kill him, Ben." I yelled. "Kill him!"

Ben had his opponent on the defensive. Then the other man gained the upper hand. With jabs, sparring, and spearing, the other man moved Ben backwards who had to kneel from the onslaught.

"Ben, clobber him!" Ben fought back, thrusting his stick into the man's face, belly, and chest. "That's it! You've got him!"

In addition to the ends of each stick being covered by padding like a boxing glove, both men wore football helmets, so neither man was in danger of being hurt. Ben stayed on the offensive and the other man fell back, using his stick to block Ben's barrage of lunges, pierces, and attacks.

"You've got him, Ben!" I yelled.

In fact, Ben's pummeling jabs overcame the skill of his opponent, and Sergeant Lucas blew his whistle to end the match. Ben could claim the victory, but I wondered how different the real thing would have been without padding or helmets and an enemy set on protecting his country from an American invasion. I didn't talk to Ben about it. It was a victory, and that was good for Fort Campbell.

We also learned to shoot our weapons like Wild Bill Hickock in a wild west show, firing BB guns at pennies thrown in the air. Amazed at how accurately we became pinging coins in midair, we picked off pennies tossed by Sergeant Lucas. We learned how to quickdraw, like in a gunfight, our guns' aim followed the pennies' trajectory in the air. Ben Gillette and I got in a shooting match. Sergeant Lucas threw a penny in the air and Ben, and I shot at it at the same time. From the sound of the ping, we knew who hit the penny and who missed. "C'mon, Ben. You missed that one."

"Oh, no. That was my kill."

"Throw another penny, Drill Sergeant."

Sergeant Lucas tossed another penny in the air, we fired our BB guns, and the ping sent the penny three feet from us. "That was my kill, too," I said.

"Hell, you missed it by a mile."

"Throw another penny, Drill Sergeant," I said. Sergeant Lucas tossed a penny right between Ben and me, we fired simultaneously, and our BBs hit the penny at the same time.

"You're getting good at this," Sergeant Lucas said. "You both hit the penny."

"One more time."

Sergeant Lucas threw a penny high in the air, we aimed our BB guns high, and the penny pinged into a trajectory to land in a group of men watching us.

"That's real marksmanship," one man said. "Who shot first?"

"I did," Ben said.

I shook my head.

Basic Training was becoming a competitive game.

At the firing range, we sighted in our M14 rifles. A second lieutenant supervised and said a good score on the range would make us "feel more betterly." I did not want to serve under this officer in Vietnam given his abuse of grammar. Second lieutenants were cannon fodder—I did not want their job.

One drill sergeant, new to his job, pulled a knife on a recruit and held it against his neck. "I could kill you with this knife." We all stood rigid, feeling what the recruit felt, the sheer fear of having a stronger human being holding a knife at his throat. We didn't know if the drill sergeant was serious or not as he held the knife to the man's throat and used his forearm to control any reaction the recruit might be compelled to make. The recruit was stone, cold still—breathless.

The sergeant really made an impression on the whole platoon. We had played around with bayonets, BB guns, and downrange targets under the watchful eyes of a training cadre whose ultimate job it was to train us so we would survive Vietnam. But this was not training. This was anger; pure emotion reacting to a recruit's smart-alec attitude. We didn't know if he would survive the sergeant's response.

The sergeant had a combat patch on his fatigues, meaning he had served in Vietnam, but to us it really meant he had been tested in combat. One slide of the knife would just mean one more notch in his professional capacity.

The crotch of the recruit's fatigues darkened with urine, and, upon seeing that bodily reaction, the sergeant relaxed his stance, grinned with an odd look in his eyes, and said. "Jesus, Recruit, get out of my sight. You wear your own piss the rest of the day, and remember this, and how easy it would have been to slice your fucking throat."

The recruit took a quick, deep breath and fought back the burning urge to cry.

"Fall in!" another drill sergeant yelled, and we immediately fell into a formation at the position of attention, suddenly realizing this was not a game at all.

And everyone of us knew—we were no longer civilians.

VIETNAM

AFTER GRADUATING FROM BASIC training, as a volunteer—instead of a draftee—I was taken care of by the Army. I had shown a natural tendency as an expert marksman that instead of being sent to Vietnam after the initial training, I was sent to Fort Polk, Louisiana as a member of the training brigade. My job? Teaching recruits—not much younger than me—to fire the Army's new weapon, the M16. I loved training and getting to handle the weapons on a live firing range, but I was a junior member on the team of trainers who would take the recruits off the hands of drill sergeants for the day, and run them through the rifle qualifications.

Most of the other trainers had combat patches indicating at least one tour in Vietnam. I didn't have that, and it stood out as

I became self-conscious about my lack of experience. Still—true to the word of my recruiter—the Infantry was the right branch for fast promotions, and in the next 19 months, I was promoted to E5, Sergeant.

Of course, I was proud of that, but my rank was pinned on my feelings of doubt. I was a great range instructor, but I had no field experience. Then with a year to go on my enlistment, that would change.

I got orders to Vietnam.

———————————• •———————————

We had been on patrol for three days, our nerves worn thin. The jungle thick around us, vines hung in our faces, trees blocked our way, and brush tore at our fatigues, as we hacked through foliage and vegetation scraping our faces. Intelligence said Charlie lurked near, so we trod delicately, crouching, fearing an ambush.

Gunderson walked point, as he always did, but today he looked down at me and complained. A corporal, a leader, the men looked up to him, and he had a protective view of them. He risked his life, every time he volunteered to walk the point. I was in command of the patrol, but the men looked to Gunderson for leadership.

Gunderson knew more than any of us why America was in Vietnam. He had studied Vietnam and its history of occupation, colonization, oppression, and the fundamental Vietnamese dislike for the Chinese. This had all provided him with insights into the justifications politicians used for sending us into the war. You'd think combat woke him to the reality of war, men and women with their entire lives ahead of them, flushed down the latrine, before their lives had started. Without bravado or the chance to see his nephew, a toddler, with whom he was close, Gunderson risked death with every step.

"Why is it always me on the point?" Shorter, I looked up at him and puffed out my chest like a peacock. From Indiana, his bravery infectious, today Gunderson balked. "I have a foreboding about this patrol."

"You never complained before. You said you were the only man you trusted on point."

"Why don't you take the point? You always take the best C-rations, best foxhole, and safest position on patrol. Are you afraid of getting hit?"

"We're all afraid of getting hit."

"Put someone else in there. I've played Russian roulette with Charlie too many times. My luck is running out."

Geiger, our radio man, from West Virginia, had the drawal of a hillbilly. A religious man, he said, "Um," and pointed to Hell, when someone swore or used the Lord's name in vain. Small and energetic, Geiger was a tunnel rat, a job that terrified me. Men crawled into the tunnels dug by the enemy out of courage and devotion to the men on the patrol.

I refused to be a tunnel rat, stating my shoulders were too wide. The duty scared me so much I stayed out of the discussion when the senior NCO picked one of us for that job.

PFC Powers wanted combat. I did not know his personal history, but concluded he picked the patrols that showed promise of encountering Charlie. Nothing scared him. With his broad shoulders, big neck, and rock jaw, he looked like a model for an Army poster. A good-natured man, he played football and wrestled in high school.

Private Smith was an artist, trained by Minneapolis College of Art and Design. He had a girlfriend back home, to whom he wrote every spare moment. She wrote to him profusely and at mail call, we watched him read letter after letter. Engaged to be married, Smith wore an engagement ring and condemned men who paid for prostitutes. He worked in oil paint, and you'd think an artist would be more understanding of the human condition.

Specialist Fourth Class Weaver was our medic. Experienced, with several patrols under his belt, he earned the badge of a combat medic. We trusted him to get us home alive. He did not wear a white cross on his helmet, a surefire target. He told us he had a tube of red lipstick in his bag to mark a cross on the forehead of a man with a tourniquet.

PFC Lewis, our biggest man, carried the M60 bandoleros for Spec 4 Hagman. He walked behind Hagman in the patrol. A college graduate, who had studied anthropology at Stanford, Lewis knew he had been lucky in life. He played football for Stanford and his father had a job waiting for him in his brokerage firm when he got home. He hated Vietnam and said so whenever the squad took a break for something to eat.

"What a stinking hell hole of a country," he said as he opened a can of ham and lima beans.

"I'll bet it's pretty if it weren't for the VC," Powers said, lighting up one of the Lucky Strikes that came in his C-rations

"It's as pretty as a latrine."

"Without the VC, it would be as pretty as those Stanford girls that saw you off."

"Those Stanford girls have high IQs."

"How did we get from latrines to Stanford girls?"

"Easy."

Hagman was our M60 man. He humped the huge machine gun up the hills and down into the gloom of the dales, its weight requiring stamina and strength. Its ammunition kept in bands looped over Lewis' shoulders, it was enough for Hagman to haul the gun itself. Hagman was a farm boy, used to hard work, and carrying the gun was like throwing a sack of potatoes.

The other men gathered around us, as I, newly promoted to sergeant, asserted myself in command. A moment I feared, taking charge, terrified of running the show. I looked up at Gunderson, swallowed, and said, "Okay." I backed down in the face of fairness and fear. "Let's get that PFC up here. What's his name?

"Whitman? He's too green, Searg."

"It's your turn. We never see you walk the point."

"I'm conserving myself. I'll do it when I'm good and ready."

"You look ready now."

"Okay," I said, my men in favor of me walking point.

I felt my way with my boots, through the plants, leaves, and bark, impenetrable between us and the VC. The rest of the men followed me. The afternoon sun slanted through the forest, in low, glowing beams angling over the jungle floor. Birds screeched; geckos hissed, and animals howled through the pitch black interior of the woods.

Then all hell broke loose. With a cacophony of flares, a barrage of shots echoing in the forest, and explosions in front of us, the VC upon us. We quickly fanned out to form a firing line, assumed a prone firing position, and returned fire, as their rounds ricocheted off tree bark below, above, and all around us. I hugged the forest floor, fired my M16 at flashes in the gloom, and threw hand grenades at the enemy, intent on slaughtering us. Pouring rounds through the jungle underbrush, we retaliated, emptying our clips, switching them, and emptying them again. M16s jumping in our arms.

Hagman and Lewis were manning the 60 beside me, laying down suppressive fire at an enemy 30 feet in front of us. Lewis fed the rounds into the chamber as they worked together as an impressive team—a proverbial well-oiled machine. The tracer rounds—every fifth round—indicated a steady leveling of the barrel shooting consistently waist- and chest-high. No enemy would risk exposure to fire into that suicidal wall of ammunition streaking downrange.

I felt a fortifying—albeit selfish—sense of protection, firing my own weapon next to that team.

"Gunderson!" I yelled, "Take the right flank!"

The ratcheting of the bursts of grenades and flashes of the enemy's AK47s filled the air, stifling us, as we laid in the undergrowth and mud, returned fire, and put up a beehive of rounds that forced them back. Then, just as suddenly as it had started, it stopped. They had retreated into the jungle with just a few shots fired from the receding distance between.

I quickly waved the back of my hand in front of my face. "Ceasefire! Ceasefire!"

A silence replaced the firefight with an eerie silence. All I could hear was my own breathing, and I caught myself longing for the natural sounds of the jungle to come back and reassure us the battle was over. "Doc," I shouted at Weaver. "Casualties?"

"We're good, Sarge," he replied back with good news.

I looked over and saw a lingering look of panic on Whitman's face. I empathized, and realized I probably had the same look. I struggled to take the mental steps to replace it with a stoic battle face.

I don't know how well I did, but found solace in not having any wounded—or KIAs.

III

A day later, an argument started between Smith and me. I ordered him to take point, but he refused, claiming it was not his turn. "Tell Geiger to take point. He hasn't done it since this patrol started."

"Geiger took over the radio when Santiago got hit. You know that."

Geiger looked at Smith, knowing he wouldn't have to take the point, but also knowing the radio made him a prime target without being on the point. Charlie was very good at wreaking havoc on logistics—like shooting up a radio, and any radioman with it on his back.

Anticipating the argumentative progression of the discussion, Gunderson intervened. "Lewis, give your 60 ammo to Whitman, and take the point."

"Alright, Guns," Lewis responded, handing the belts of 7.62mm ammo to the new guy.

Resentment for the corporal boiled up over my realization that I should have been able to handle the conversation better. I knew Sergeant First Class (SFC) Teller, the Platoon Sergeant, had witnessed the exchange, and I felt a lack of competence overcome me. It was my role as squad leader to give assignments, fairly and with conviction. It was the duty of my rank, and I wasn't good at it at all.

I knew the squad knew it as well.

"Move out, Second Squad!" SFC Teller boomed at me.

With the most to lose, but with confidence, Lewis walked toward death, his eyes looking for booby traps and boots feeling for pits in the trail potentially filled with punji sticks. I admired his skill. He had been in-country nine months and was an experienced professional at a job that required professional expertise.

The kind I didn't have.

Lewis had his weapon at sling arms as he hacked through the brush with a machete to clear a path for the squad. We followed him, in single file, the plants, trees, and bushes wrapping around our fatigues along the edge of the cleared path. Each machete swing opened vistas of darkness in the jungle where water dripped from leaves, wetting our fatigues. Our helmets echoed the scraping of the greenery across their protective cover, as we plunged deeper into the engulfing woods.

After about 40 minutes of patrolling the jungle, Lewis stopped, held up his free hand, crouched, and looked back at us. The squad halted and squatted with anticipation trusting Lewis' judgment.

He motioned for us to spread out, stay low and take cover. And, as if on command, the jungle erupted into a ratcheting of rounds.

I quickly took a defensive position behind a fallen log and started firing blindly. The rest of the squad took similar action, and we were quickly in the mindless fever of a firefight aiming at widely dispersed flashes as the enemy showered us with AK47 rounds.

A hand grenade rolled toward me, and for an ungodly, senseless reason, I thought it looked like a grape wobbling, but in the same instant, my mind took over and had enough mindful wherewithal to pick it up and throw it back. It exploded in the air.

I regained a certain degree of faith in myself, and yelled, "Gunderson, watch the left. Smith! Right flank!"

The men poured clip after clip into Charlie's realm. Our rounds emptied from their thirty round magazine duct taped together to quickly be flipped for easier reloading.

In the sound of it all, the senselessness returned to me, and my mind left the scene altogether, suddenly seeing a line of ducks flying over a duck blind. I shook my head violently in an effort to refocus, and I was back in the firefight with a feeling of being the only one the VC were shooting at. That feeling came with a considerable amount of fear, but I squeezed off rounds in a three-round burst, trying not to waste ammo.

Then, it was over.

The VC had retreated like jungle spirits into the dark as our firing turned from full blast to sporadic to silent. The call for a ceasefire came up the line, but another call came as well.

"Medic!" Powers yelled, and Weaver ran to him, pulling something out of his medic bag.

He shouted to me, "Sucking chest wound!" I watched Weaver take a square sheet of plastic, tape it over the hole in Powers' chest, and place the man in the shock position to protect his brain and prevent further loss of blood.

"You bastards!" I yelled.

"We sent 'em runnin', Sarge!" Smith yelled.

"You sons of bitches!" I yelled with a mix of bravado and fear swirling through me and taking control of my mind. The senseless rationale, dreamlike now, took over again. For some reason, I thought of fish; the VC were like a school of fish swimming away from my pole. My M16 turned into a fishing rod. It was ridiculous. I knew it was ridiculous, but it made sense. I took the stock of my M16 and held it like a fishing rod, casting it, but laughing when I let go of it. It splashed into the mud right beneath where the grenade had exploded in air. I fought myself to gain composure, but all I could do was stop laughing. I could see ducks and fish, and they turned around at me, quacking and gaping, and saying, "We sent 'em runnin', Sarge!"

Then I collapsed. I watched myself go over the edge, into the abyss, where senselessness reigned, worse than the chaos in the firefight. I saw my mother's acorn squash, my father's Manhattan, my sister's school blouse, my brother's beer, and his wife's hand on his hand. The glass chandelier sparkled in the sun beaming through the bay window.

"We sent 'em runnn', Sarge!" echoed from those images. I nodded, but none of it made sense. I had a sudden realization that none of it mattered. None of it had anything to do with me.

I was unable to move, speak, or care.

"Sergeant Reynolds is down," Gunderson said. "Who else is hurt?"

"Powers. He's hurt bad."

"Call for medevac."

"Bravo Six," Geiger said on the radio, "this is Bravo Two. Come in, Bravo Six, over."

"Bravo Two," the radio sparked back, "this is Bravo Six, send your traffic, over."

"Roger, Bravo Six, we are requesting a MEDEVAC, three clicks north of Firebase Lima, over."

"Roger, Bravo Two, send your coordinates, over."

"Reynolds had a breakdown," Weaver told Gunderson. "I can't see anything wrong with him, but he's not moving or talking. He just froze up, best I can tell."

"How about Powers?" Gunderson asked.

"We gotta get him out of here quick. He's struggling to breathe. Sucking chest wound," Weaver replied.

"Chopper's on the way to that clearing, thirty yards back," Geiger informed Gunderson.

"Powers took a bullet in the chest," Gunderson told the medic onboard the helicopter. "And Reynolds just froze up."

The medic nodded, secured Powers and me on the floor of the helo behind the door gunner, and gave the pilot a thumb's up. We lifted out of the jungle.

And I joined the ducks in my new reality.

HOME

HOME FROM VIETNAM SIX months before my tour was up, terrified of my own shadow, I hid in my room, with the stereo and TV. I drove to Minneapolis to bar hop, until I was drunk, searched for my car for an hour, and drove home drunk.

As the months passed, that directionless routine helped me escape the homelife of mowing my father's lawn, shoveling his sidewalk, and making my bed. I would come home late, the room spinning, throw up in the toilet, pass out, sleep poorly, and do it all again the next day. I grew my beard out, let my hair grow, and wore a leather motorcycle-club vest—all which angered my father, who wanted me to transition to civilian life, the way he did after WWII.

Ours was a relationship connected by and to the same American military, the same volunteer experience, the same sense of service—but we had two totally different perspectives on what honor, duty, and country really meant. So, we struggled to reconcile our attitudes split between the welcome-home-parades of "the class of '42" and the I-survived-a year "class of '68."

And what made it all worse was the fact I didn't survive my year.

AFTERMATH

APPOINTMENT AND APPOINTMENT, THERE followed years of psychiatry and pills. Pills when I woke, again at noon, and again at bedtime. Psychiatry was routine, and routinely futile. My doctors changed my medication five times. I developed tremors from taking one drug for too long—more tremors from not taking another drug long enough. My mother's edict to never miss an appointment and always take my pills did not override my pursuit of a cure using the outdoors.

"Does the shaking come and go?" asked one doctor.

"Yes. Today the tremors aren't bad."

"Are your hands steady when you put them on your knees?"

"Yes. But if I let them hang, the shaking starts."

"The nurse said they are no worse than last month."

"My friends think they are worse."

"I'll leave your medication where it is, and we'll check it again in five months."

In the meantime, I shook like I had Saint Vitus Dance and people thought I had Parkinson's Disease.

"Mike, you have *one* job," my father said. "To get well. Your mother and I don't care if you don't work."

"I'm using the outdoors to get well," I declared.

"The VA, too," my mother said. "I talked to your doctor. He said you are making good progress."

"Doctor Jonas? He treats me like I've got a brain in my head. Some of those doctors think everything I say is bullshit."

"Watch your language in front of your mother."

"I'm going skiing in Alta this year."

"If you think it will help, we'll pay for it."

"Sit up," my mother said. "Your posture is terrible. Be proud of yourself. Breakdowns happen."

"I'm proud of myself, Mom."

"I know you are."

Along with my medical rehabilitation, Vietnam plagued me. Memories recurred, and I condemned soldiers in a constant comparison projected on their service. I considered my sacrifice more … I don't know—worthy? Sacrificial? I judged them as not having paid their dues. Even the ones with missing limbs. At least they weren't shaking and could hold onto clear thoughts long enough to have conversations—and relationships.

Nightmares of firefights woke me up sweating and screaming in the night. No. That's not right. It was a voice that woke me up.

"We sure sent 'em runnin' Sarge!"

"We sure sent 'em runnin'!"

Sometimes it was Smith's voice, sometimes it was a collective quack of a flock of ducks flying over the canopy of jungle. Then, sometimes, it was Ben Gillette, dressed in fatigues and a football helmet, carrying a pugil stick while running into and being torn apart by a wall of AK47 ammo. Ben had, in reality, been killed in action in Operation Toan Thang II not too long after we graduated from Basic Training—about a month after he arrived in Vietnam. I was at Fort Polk in Tiger Land when I found out. In those Ben Gillette dreams, along with the scream and the sweat, I also woke up with a heavy burden of guilt.

In other nightmare scenes I was looking down on myself about walking along a trail in the jungle, suddenly rolling to take cover against the ambush of weapons blazing, and then—in the middle of combat—I could see the Viet Cong sliding down vines out of the trees, sitting next to me, smiling, and drinking out of my canteen. Awake, it was worse. My mind and body were elastic bands, pulled like Silly Putty stretched on a three-dimensional rack—left, right, up, down—all at the same time. And in those stretched out moments when I was physically and mentally a sheet of paper, longing to be ripped to ease the tension, I could hear the men in the platoon calling me, "Reynolds, we need you!"

"We need you, Sarge!"

I saw them all around me, lying face down in rice paddies, or dark shadowy figures standing in formation.

"We need you!"

When I could shake those visions, and when I woke up from the nightmares, I would go into my parents' kitchen, grab a beer, and sit at our kitchen table. Sometimes I would think of the chemical reaction between drugs and alcohol, but most times, I just drank to not be able to think at all.

Loud noises, like backfires from cars, children yelling in the park, firecrackers, or even a car door slamming, put me on edge, and I insisted on sitting with my back to the wall in restaurants, coffee shops, and waiting rooms.

When I wasn't living with my parents, I would try to live alone in apartments where I kept the lights off, struggled to settle my nerves, ignored the messes I made, and physically shook while my mind waited for another round of alcohol—any alcohol—to take control. It could be hard liquor, beer, or even, in some of my lowest moments of locked away instability, isopropyl alcohol with the edge taken off of it with table salt.

ATTEMPTS AT GETTING WELL

DESPITE MY CYNICISM TOWARD America, my distaste for society, and my frequent escapes with a growing problem of alcoholism, I had not given up on myself and actually wanted to get well. It may have been bad faith lying to myself, but underneath the image I was trying to maintain was an identity wanting to get out—to recover.

My parents, when I had dinner with them, talked about getting me "fixed." This meant "well" and their marching orders to me were to devote all my effort to my recovery. They did not care what it cost and, whether they could afford it or not, they paid for the skiing trips recommended by the VA.

They were very supportive. My mother was always upbeat and encouraging—even when I was drunk and belligerent. And my father, though he hated my beard, long hair, and black motorcycle-gang vest, respected to the hilt my time in the Army and my tour in Vietnam.

Although, he hated my mental illness so much that I thought he hated me.

When he introduced me to his business associates, he did it reluctantly, proud I was a Vietnam veteran, but hating my unkempt appearance. His partners sat in our living room, in suit and tie, and my skin and bones in my black leather vest looked like a cadaver about to be dissected and examined by a group of med students.

To keep my mother happy, I never missed an appointment with my psychiatrist at the VA and always took my pills.

At the VA, I walked tall, with a projected look of healing capacities for the doctors and nurses trying to help me, although it reverted back to the "fuck-this" look I thought helped portray me as a victim of the war to help me fit in with the other patients—who wore that look naturally, or else portrayed it was well as I thought I was projecting it.

"You've had a serious emotional problem," my doctor told me one day. Indeed, it had gotten to the point we could finally talk about it.

"I'm well aware of that."

"Do you think you have been feeling better?"

"Yes. My feelings are more settled. I'm warm and fuzzy now."

"You don't have to be a wiseass. We're trying to help you."

"I am feeling much better. My breathing is even better. Not as erratic or prone to stress."

"We'll keep you on the same dose of Haldol. I know you don't like it. I don't like it either. But it's working. Let's not rock the boat."

"If I stop taking Haldol, I end up back in the psych ward."

"That's right. And you start all over."

"I haven't had an erection in three years."

"The side effects should wear off by now."

"I need a date to test it."

"Don't look at me. I can't help you. I'm a psychiatrist. You might consider an understanding woman, but don't do anything to embarrass me or the VA."

"I have an old girlfriend in mind. I'll call her."

"Make sure you clean yourself up. You have a tendency to stink."

I nodded, wondering who else I had offended by being less than hygienic.

I called the girl—an old acquaintance from my college days—who agreed to go out with me. I bought her an African lobster tail dinner, the most expensive thing on the menu, but she decided I was too fucked up to sleep with. My illness permeated my face, speech, and mannerisms, and she found nothing attractive about me. I gesticulated more than was necessary when I talked, was overly effusive, and repeated myself, not coming to the point, until I had said the same thing three times, differently each time.

I'm still not sure she would have helped my erectile issues anyway.

Occasionally, I saw other old friends, and sometimes we would hang out at Dunn Brothers Coffee Shop. Just when I thought they were tolerating my appearance—and hopefully, my odor—one of them asked, "When are you going to shave that beard? You've been back for a while. How long is the rebellion going to last?"

"Sometimes I don't think I'm back at all," I confessed, surprising myself for opening up more than I wanted to. "Vietnam is right now. I live in it every day."

"You're an anachronism. A magnificent anachronism, like Patton."

I didn't even know what being an "anachronism" meant. Which made me wish I had stayed in school and taken that class on big words. I looked around to hide my ignorance. I stuck out in the coffee shop surrounded by college students and retirees.

"You're not eating right, either. Look at you. You're skin and bones."

"I eat what I need. I'm at my military weight."

"Your friends care about you. You go to the VA, but are they helping you? You never seem to get better."

"I get better every day. I can feel it. I feel myself improve each day, just a bit but enough to keep me going."

"If you say so."

"It's what I live for. God does not want me sick."

"So it's in God's hands now, is it? I didn't know Jack Daniels came with a New Testament."

CAMP

MY FATHER WAS A bank president and entrepreneur who pioneered small aircraft financing in the Midwest. He flew an airplane, belonged to three country clubs, and drove a Cadillac, all paid for by the bank. Often, in hopes of motivating me to get back into society, he introduced me to business associates. He was proud of my service, but hated my appearance and my attitude.

After one of my appointments with the VA, I met Sam. He was a Vietnam veteran who rated medications for his own condition—I was never sure what his condition actually was—and he invited me to a camp—a makeshift community—to meet other veterans who had cashed in their chips and decided bivouacking in a local woods was better than working, going to school, or having to put up with the peace-minded attitudes that persecuted their previous decisions and circumstances.

"I'm moving out," I told my parents over dinner one night.

"Where are you going?" The evening sun poured through the bay window, lighting the glass chimneys on the needlepoint runner on the table.

"To a camp in the woods."

"What kind of camp?"

"A tent camp."

"What will you do in the winter?" The impact of my decision had not registered with them, and hearing "camp" made them think of me as a twelve-year-old going off for a week in the summer.

"We have heaters. I'll have my sleeping bag."

"In twenty-five degrees below zero weather?"

The backyard glowed deep green, illuminated by the setting sun, and the windows of our neighbor's house lit brightly.

"Sam said they handled it."

"Who's Sam?"

"The leader of the camp."

"What about the VA?"

Our entire house was lit by the sunlight from the bay window in the kitchen. The ham dinner, with scalloped potatoes, glistened in the slanting rays of the setting sun.

"I'll stick with my treatment. You know that."

"That's all we care about. What does your psychologist think of this idea?"

"She doesn't like it."

"We don't like it either. You won't be safe in the woods. How will you eat?" My father speared a slice of ham from the plate in the middle of the table.

"We cook our own food."

The sunset deepened and the lawn darkened, shadows lengthened, casting our Currier and Ives part of town into early night.

"On what? A campfire like a Boy Scout?" He took a bite of the ham, chewed it as he talked, and followed it with a piece of pineapple.

"No," I corrected him. "Like Infantry soldiers."

"How about laundry?" my mother intervened.

"The river," I stated.

My mother ate the potatoes and cut the pineapple; too distracted by the conversation to remark about how well the meal had come out.

"Mike," my father said, putting down his knife and fork, "ever since you came home from Vietnam, your mother and I have worried about you. We have tried to help you. We both feel you need to be on your own. Living at home has not worked. If you live in the camp, we will worry about you, but you have to live your own life. You will make your own decisions. Living at home is not good for you, but as long as you are safe there, your mother and I won't force you to stay. Not that we could."

"Thanks, Dad. Mom not to worry about me. I'll stay warm and eat well. I need to get away. All I do now is drink."

"That's all you want to do."

"That's all I think I can do. So, I need the outdoors. I'm too old to mow your lawn or shovel your sidewalk for an allowance and meals."

"You know you can always come back."

"Thank you for understanding. I'm leaving tomorrow."

"Oh, Sweetie. I don't like this idea. I'll send you off with a nice meatloaf."

The sunset was complete, dusk fell, the neighborhood streetlights coming on, and the neighbor's window lost its shine.

———————————• •———————————

I met Sam at the public access to Crosby Lake Park, a cul de sac circled by a low wall of limestone with a few parked cars owned by the people taking a walk in the warm fall weather. A nondescript man, handsome if you liked gentle features, of medium height, lithe build, Sam had an easy voice with a hint of a Southern drawl. Narrow shoulders with a slight stoop portrayed a nonathletic man.

A 173rd Airborne Division infantryman in Vietnam, he tried to get back into the service when his civilian job in construction fell through, but for reasons unknown, they wouldn't take him. He was married with two children but had traded that family for alcohol.

A leader, Sam supervised the camp with a gentle hand and looked forward to including me in the camp, as another drinking buddy, and fellow Vietnam veteran. Loaded half the time, Sam spent the majority of the other half of the time in his tent, sleeping off a bender.

He escorted me to the camp, down a long asphalt pathway, past Crosby Lake full of lily pads, ducks, geese, and a swamp on the other side of the path of moss, fallen logs, algae, and decayed trees. We walked a long way, past cottonwoods hundreds of years old, soaring hundreds of feet to a canopy of leaves blocking the sun. Then Sam stepped off the path, into the woods, at an entrance unidentifiable with the rest of the forest. He led the way, under overhanging trees, past brush with thorns my vest protected me from, and over logs we straddled to cross. We weaved in the woods, changed directions, then came to a man in a green T-shirt, camouflaged in the woods, a sentinel who let us pass into the camp of small and low tents, each fit for one person, with no visible profile. Several people were in the camp, taking clothes off a clothesline, eating out of a can that looked like Dinty Moore Stew, or tipping up the last of a bottle—beer, whiskey, gin, vodka; whatever. Sam showed me to my tent, a red, nylon affair with mosquito netting, and a double roof, to protect the inside from rain, where I threw my backpack, and pulled out my mother's meatloaf to share with the others.

"The man living in this tent left last week and never returned," Sam said.

Sam, looking for company, dragging people down, corrupting them, thought alcohol was the only solution to a shared veteran's plight. The camp was pervasively inhabited by alcoholics, mostly pickled between waking to sleeping.

Sam admitted people and kicked them out arbitrarily, mostly for not paying their way for the booze. Sam did not like moochers and evicted them if they tried to drink for free. Honor among drunks, each person in the camp proved solvency to pay for liquor. Sam supervised this camp life, and being broke assured dismissal from the camp. "Pay or pull," Sam called it, meaning people had to pay for the alcohol or pull their weight in chores. Liquor made the camp go round, not homelessness, veteran status, or unemployment.

I fit right in.

CAMP LIFE

WHEN I WOKE UP the next morning, I stepped out of my tent and heard nothing in the camp, except the snoring of men. They had passed out and seemed dead, except for the rise and fall of their chests and the sound of their exhalations. They lay on their sides, their arms under them. They wore parkas smudged with dirt and their long hair hung scraggly and unkempt.

The tents circled the cooking area, several Sterno cans stood in the middle of the camp, their pink interiors blackened from use. Around the cooking area, in front of the tents, were logs that took the place of furniture. Cigarette butts scattered the ground, and crushed beer cans littered the area. A few off-brand alcohol bottles lay empty on their sides and a black garbage bag held beer cans to its limit.

"Where are you from?" I was startled by the voice interrupting the otherwise snoring-silent scene of the morning. I looked over and saw a man sitting on the ground in front of a log, caringly rolling a cigarette. A woman on the log looked up at me—she might have smiled at me, but I wouldn't swear to it.

"Right here. My parents live on the hill." I sat down on another log angled to their left.

"What street?"

"Montcalm Place."

"That is definitely the hill." The man handed the rolled cigarette to a woman sitting on one of the logs.

"What brings you here?" she asked leaning forward into a Zippo lighter the man had flicked open and sparked into a flame.

"I've had it. Nothing works. Living at home doesn't work. You know how it is."

"Yeah, I guess we do. Fucking war. Took it all out of us," the man said, beginning to roll another cigarette for himself. "We don't owe the world a thing."

"Why do you live here instead of in town?" I asked.

"One, who has that money? But, two, we like it here. We're all friends. We can drink ourselves to death and no one notices."

"I need the outdoors." I raised my arms, pointed in all directions.

"You'll get plenty of that here. What outfit were you in?"

"First Cavalry."

"You saw a lot of action."

I nodded slightly, hesitating to tell them very many details.

"I was a company clerk in Plie Ku. You know Sam made the only parachute jump in Vietnam."

"Was he on it? I heard about it," I said, then asked, "What was the military purpose of that jump?"

"Ask Sam. He was at the briefing. I think a general got a wild hair up his ass."

"What about the women here?"

"A wide mix—some veterans; some sympathetic hippie chicks trying to convert us back into pacifists. They're hard to fuck, but they'll stick by you if you do. Do you want a smoke?" He held up the cigarette he rolled.

"What about you?" I asked the woman.

"I'm hard to fuck," she responded.

"No, I meant…"

"I know what you meant. I was a volunteer with the Red Cross—out of Saigon."

"Really?"

"Don't sound so surprised," she said.

"I'm sorry … I didn't know…"

"Very few people do," she cut me off.

"Hey, you want a beer?" The man asked from behind his cigarette.

"I'd love a beer," I said, thankful to be reprieved from my ignorance of Red Cross volunteers.

"There's some beer in our tent. Help yourself." He pointed to the green tent behind him and to the right—just next to my red tent.

I grabbed a Cold Spring, cheap as it got, that tasted like elm leaves, and downed it in one gulp.

"Man, that's terrible," I said.

"It's not bad for around here," the man smiled.

VICKY

I HEARD A WOMAN'S LAUGHTER, awoke startled, crawled out of my tent, and saw Vicky, the girl who had joined us at Jackson Hole. She looked a little older, but no worse for wear, and I recognized her right away. Though I can't say she remembered me.

She wore her blonde hair in a ponytail, stuck through a baseball cap, and the holes in her blue jeans showed she liked comfort over fashion. Her sweatshirt read Concordia University and hung to her knees. She smiled at me, but still without recognition, and her level eyes penetrated me with a spellbound gaze. She joined us on the log we used for a couch and struck up a conversation about the Wilhelm Dairy Farm where she worked. She lit a cigarette from the hard pack of Marlboros she kept in her pants pocket. I offered her a beer, and she took it, tilting back the can and downing it in one gulp that made her throat convulse.

"I take care of one hundred cows. Milk them, feed them, water them, and put them in the pasture. It takes all day to get my work done. It's outdoors, my only job requirement."

"Do you have a barn and sling hay?"

"Yes, I do that, too. No money in it. I need a raise, or I won't be able to make it. Living on student loans right now."

"You don't remember me, do you?" I finally asked.

She studied my face, but still failed the test.

"Jackson Hole. Three years ago. No. Closer to four years now."

"Wait a minute. Matt? No, Mack," she said.

"Mike," I corrected.

"Oh, sure. The Army guy. Did you join?"

"Oh, yes," I replied.

"How was it?"

"A picnic," I said, drenching it with as much sarcasm as I could muster.

"I bet," she replied. "Are you out now?"

"Yeah. I've been out for about 6 months now."

"How have you been?"

"I'm okay," I lied, hesitating to tell her too many details to scare her away from my renewed infatuation.

"What have you been doing?" she asked.

"Transitioning," I replied, wanting to immediately change the subject. "But how have you been? Where did you go after Jackson Hole?"

"I got a job in a hospital and hated it. It was indoors, and I hated it."

"What were you doing in a hospital?"

"Counseling. I was a Family Studies major."

"Really? How was that?"

"Let's just say I would rather study cows than families," she replied with just a hint of a smile giving away a personal inside joke.

The woods surrounded us, the Mississippi River half a mile away, and birds sang from the Cottonwoods soaring above. The tents held sleeping campers whose feet stuck out of them, and the rest of us sat on the log and drank. A couple of men entered the camp with backpacks full of bottles of vodka, bourbon, and six packs of beer.

"We're not cavemen. We have tents, food, cigarettes, booze, and each other."

"Can I move in here?" Vicky asked.

"Not if you're working. It's too long a walk to Shepherd Road to get to your car. The cops would find it."

"I'll visit then. It's okay to park in the circle."

"You can't leave your car there overnight. Well, you can, but it may not be there in the morning. They close the gate at eight. Park in the high-rise lot. We're friends with the cop who lives there. Sam can talk to him."

"What brought you here?" she asked.

"Sam said it was a safe place to drink. Help yourself to the beer. Throw your empties in that garbage bag."

"Makes sense," she smiled, putting her first empty beer can in the garbage bag.

"Why Wilhelm Dairy Farm?" I asked, shifting my attention and genuine interest back to her.

"Why not? A lot of it is indoors milking cows. But a lot of it is outdoors putting the cows to pasture."

"A happy cow is a productive cow. Is that it?"

"Yes. I spend a lot of time cleaning cow pies, but the boss said I'd get promoted to herder. I'll believe it when I see it. The farm has been in the family for five generations."

"No chance for advancement."

"At least I'm outdoors. The boss gives me outdoors jobs, painting the barn, repairing the fence, and cleaning the equipment."

Vicky came to see us every weekend, and always spent the night. We slept in my sleeping bag, platonically, holding each other to stay warm, then one night I asked if I could kiss her. She said, yes, I held her in the sleeping bag, and we made love, long, everlasting, never ending, ongoing, never stopping, keeping forever love.

Vicky made people feel good—made me feel good. Her innate intelligence propelled her through a degree with honors at a private college. Her love of other people and faith in herself and her father jettisoned her through situations others shook off. She took them to heart. A conversation gone bad, a relationship turned sour, or a farm animal untended, threw her into a tizzy taking days to reverse. She did not need to talk, even say, hi, for her beneficial effect to take hold. A human lightbulb, heat lamp, beacon, and lighthouse, she gave people value unawares, their place in life fixed, resigned, and happy to be there, knowing their just reward for conduct warranted.

Denizen of another planet, Vicky came to earth to preach peace, love of others, and she poured forth light, beauty, and warmth. Her blue jeans with holes in the knees, serape covering her shoulders, black and blue mark where a horse kicked her, baseball cap with her ponytail stuck through it, betrayed a woman above it all.

She descended like an angel to earth to bring love to us lucky enough to know her, her serape was her set of wings.

PARENTS

I TOOK VICKY HOME TO meet my parents. I wanted to show her I was serious about her and show my parents the girl I had looked for all my life. Unlike every other girl I slept with, I cared about Vicky.

First, we stopped at J. R. Mac's for a drink, where I prepared her for a shock. We ordered Manhattans in the wooden floored bar where only two other people were sitting in the booth in the corner. They were holding hands. The bartender wore an argyle sweater tucked in old blue jeans held up by a worn leather belt.

"I come from an unusual family," I said as I leaned on the bar.

"Your father is an accountant, and your mother is a wing walker, I suppose." She fondled her drink and looked up at me playfully.

"No. My father was a Naval officer in WWII and the Korean War. He was a Beach Jumper."

"What's a Beach Jumper?"

"They go in before the landing craft."

"Sounds dangerous."

"They use scuba gear. Attach mines to the hulls of enemy ships. Another name for them is Frogmen."

"Spare me. What about your mother?"

"She studies ballet and has a solo private airplane license."

"At least they're not in the circus, taming lions, and riding elephants." She leaned on the bar with thought and twirled the cherry in her drink.

"No, but they love to entertain and are socially prominent in town."

"Now, I'm nervous. I'll be on my best behavior."

Fortified by drinks, we took the Seventh Street bus to the Lexington Avenue bus that dropped us two blocks from my parents' home. We walked along their street, Vicky shocked at the opulence of the homes and view of downtown St. Paul. We came to my parents' house—two stories, newly painted gray, with an attached garage on a slight hill, my father's sprinkler system watering the lawn I hated to mow. We walked up the long steps, and I rang the doorbell.

My mother answered, wide eyed, not expecting us. I had lost so much weight in the two months since I left home, I wondered if she would even recognize me. But of course—a mother doesn't forget her children.

She smiled, standing at the open door. "Mike! Come in! Who's your friend?"

"Mom, this is Vicky. Vicky, this is my mother."

"Hi, Vicky. Welcome! You can call me Anne." My mother shook Vicky's hand. "Mike, show her around. Have you had dinner? I made chili and cornbread before we played golf. It's in the fridge. I can heat it up."

"We'd like that, Mom. We're hungry."

Vicky could not believe the house, with its living room rug salvaged from the dining room of the Minnesota Club when it was remodeled, hardwood floors my father refinished, fieldstone fireplace, three bay windows, wallpaper printed with ducks and geese my father put up, the dining room table with a needlepoint runner, two stone chimneys, and a glass chandelier above the table—the décor expensive and tasteful.

My father came in, poured himself a drink, and started chatting with Vicky who was dazzled by the cornucopia of the liquor cabinet, from red, black, and green bottles of aperitifs to Wild Turkey to Seagram's Crown Royal, still in its velvet jacket. My mother had painted rosemaling in oil on the door of the liquor cabinet that had been converted from being an armoire for precious clothing.

"What'll you two have? I can make you anything," my father boasted.

Vicky stepped to the bar to admire the collection of liquor. "I'll have scotch and soda, please."

"Johnny Walker Black, okay?"

"I'll say."

"I'll have the same thing," I said.

Vicky felt familiar with my father. He stepped to the kitchen, opened the refrigerator, took out an ice cube tray, and cracked the cubes into the cork ice bucket.

"As you wish," he called. Back in the living room, he made Vicky a scotch and soda and handed it to her.

"Dave, I'll have a drink, too," my mother called from the kitchen. "A toddy for the body."

We sat in the living room and sipped our drinks.

"Vicky works on the Wilhelm Dairy Farm," I said.

"That's a lot of work," my father said. "Our daughter-in-law owns a horse. Our other son's wife."

"What kind?"

"Mike, you tell her."

"Western saddle bred."

"That's a nice horse. Our cows at the dairy are Holsteins, Brown Swiss, and Red Angus." A little nervous, she sat on the couch with her legs crossed, holding her glass on her knee, her erect posture like a lady interviewing for a job.

My father took a sip of his drink, then asked, "Where are you skiing this year?"

"Alta, Utah. Greatest powder snow on the planet."

The evening sun poured in the bay window that looked onto the back yard, a natural fence of little pine trees, and our neighbor's house with a greenhouse of orchids in their back yard.

"How much do you make working at a dairy?" my father asked.

"Dad," I objected.

"It's alright," Vicky responded, obviously relaxing in the surroundings. "I make minimum wage—a dollar-sixty."

"You'll get more. Refresher?" Dad asked and got up to make himself another drink.

"Please." Vicky held out her glass, and I stepped to the liquor cabinet and offered him my empty glass as well. My father fixed Vicky and me another scotch and soda and a Manhattan for him.

"What do your parents do?" Dad asked, back in his chair, legs crossed, glass on the armrest, checking Vicky's pedigree. He smiled as he talked to Vicky, loving to entertain her, and pleased with her answers.

"It's just my dad. He's in electronics."

"With whom?"

"He's been with Hart Ski Company since he came back from Korea."

"He was in Korea?" my dad asked.

"Yes. When I was just a baby. In '51."

"You're still a baby," my father smiled, obviously flirting now.

"Damned wars," my mother interjected. "They tear families apart more than anything else. Look at Mike. How are you coming along, Mike?"

"I saw my psychologist last week."

"Is it still the woman doctor? What did she say?"

"Yeah—the same one. She just wanted to know about the camp."

"Don't mess with the VA, and get all you can from them," my father said.

"That's right, Mike, You deserve all you can get from them," my mother said, then disappeared into the kitchen to reemerge with the cornbread and chili on a tray with the food distributed in Mexican pottery.

"Anne loves the Spicks," my father announced when he saw the pottery. "She goes to Mexico every year. She speaks Spanish. Taught herself."

"They are Mexicans," my mother reprimanded my father, knowing the alcohol had started loosening an unfiltered tongue. "My Spanish is rusty, but I can get by in the market."

"I had a roommate who was a Mexican exchange student in school," Vicky told them.

"Vicky was on a scholarship at Concordia." The liquor took its effect on me, and I lay back, loosening up on the couch.

"This looks wonderful," Vicky said. "A home cooked meal."

"Nothing fancy. Just threw it together. Vicky, is your mother alive?"

"Died five years ago. Just before I met Mike in Jackson Hole."

"Oh, I'm sorry," my mother said.

"It's okay. We were never really close," Vicky deflected.

"You met Mike in Jackson Hole?" my father asked, accepting the deflection.

"Yes. Four years ago. We just happened to meet again at the camp. Total coincidence."

"Are you done with school?" my mother asked, not wanting to hear about the camp.

"Oh, yes. I graduated with a degree in Family Studies."

"And you're working on a farm?" my father questioned.

Vicky smiled. "The herd is like a family. Maybe not as complex."

"Complex. That's a good word," I said.

"And besides, I would rather be outside than working in some counselor's office in a hospital," Vicky diverted away from a discussion on families hitting too close to home.

"Happiness is worth it," my mother said to Vicky, leaning back from the TV dinner table in front of the chair with a broad back and big armrests.

"Another drink?" my father asked.

"Oh, no. That was enough, and what a nice match with the meal, Mrs—Anne," Vicky said, catching her manners resuming back to the safe side of best behavior.

"Every good man's fault," my father said, referring to his glass as he got up to mix another Manhattan. "Mike is a Jekyll and Hyde when he drinks."

"That's a good excuse to quit," my mother said.

"I like the stuff, happy or not," I mumbled. Then added, "Great chili, Mom."

"You can come home any time. Even just for dinner. You're welcome here, too, Vicky. Any time. You two seem to get along."

"Thanks, Anne. You have a beautiful home. It's very comfortable."

"Thank you. We do it ourselves." She began picking up the bowls and plates and taking them to the kitchen.

Vicky offered to help, but my mom refused. "It's okay, I'll stick them in the dishwasher later."

Our dog, a Cairn terrier, entered the room, came up to Vicky, and sniffed the cuff of her jeans. Vicky leaned over and petted the dog. "What's the dog's name?"

"Dinah," I said. "Short for Dynamite."

"Get down, Dinah," my father scowled. "Get off the couch. You know better than that."

The dog jumped off the couch and ran to my mother who picked her up and held the dog in her lap.

"I love animals," Vicky said. "My job is ideal. I get paid to work with my favorite animals."

"She puts the farm animals to bed, waters them, pastures them, and gives them blankets. Even in the dead of winter. She works until eight at night."

"It's cold at that time of night."

"How do you treat the cows in the winter?"

"Cows run warmer than people, so we lower the shades in the barn and let them lie down in their stalls. They get along fine."

"Dad, we better get going. They will close the gate to the park soon. Thanks for having us."

"You just got here!" My mother came out of the kitchen wringing her hands in a dish towel.

"Got to get back to the camp before it gets too dark to find it. Park rangers close the gate at eight. Vicky needs sleep before work tomorrow. She starts at five thirty."

"You don't need to stay in that camp. Neither one of you. Vicky, if you ever feel unsafe there, you come here," my mother said.

"Oh, it's okay. I have Mike. And there's no danger. But thank you," Vicky said.

My mother hugged us both goodbye, and my father shook my hand then Vicky's.

"We look forward to seeing you again."

They stood in the doorway as we walked down the long steps.

Vicky and I stepped into the warm fall evening and, deciding we had time to walk instead of taking the bus, we began the long walk down the hill to the camp. A slight breeze cooled our armpits and caressed our faces.

"You bowled them over," I said.

"I love them."

"Nice, aren't they?"

"Yes. Kind, too. I wish my father could meet them."

We turned onto Lexington Avenue and walked along a neighborhood of modest homes and towering oaks, red in their fall colors.

NAMEKAGON RIVER

MY FATHER SPENT SUMMERS in his childhood near Cable, Wisconsin, a fisherman's paradise with lakes and streams loaded with walleye, trout, muskies, and northern pike. He took me there, three hours north of the Twin Cities, hoping the outdoors in that area would help cure me of my schizoaffective disorder, or least ease the symptoms. My father said he would cut off his balls to help me, so taking me fishing on a weekend in Cable was a small thing.

The surface of Lake Namekagon shone like molten glass in the sun. Although we were below the dam, and the lake was six feet above us. The water poured over the dam, and into the pool where we were fishing.

The woods were all around us except for the clearing the forest service had made for a campsite. The pool was deep and churned slightly from the current and our fishing lines cut the water from the movement. Longtime friends of my father, Jack and Nancy, fished from the shore. Jack was a carpenter and Nancy worked in the bank.

We were fishing for walleyes, but below the lake, I knew to use a fly rod because I was more likely to catch pike. Besides, I liked the fight the more aggressive pike fish would give on the line. I hooked something, and the fly rod dipped, then jerked. The rod was bent over, and the fish cleared the water. A northern. A two pounder.

"Hey, Jack," I yelled. "There isn't a walleye in here to save your ass!"

"You're catching fish, aren't you?" Jack yelled back from the shore. "Don't complain. Just keep fishing. We'll pickle the northern. And there are walleyes here. So just keep fishing and keep your mouth shut."

"That Jack's something else," my father said, from the bow of the canoe.

"He thinks he's an expert," I said. "Hasn't been a walleye caught in here in a million years."

"You're probably right," my father said. "But don't tell him."

"If he hadn't talked us into fishing this hole, we could be halfway down the river with a mess of trout in the creel."

"What the hell," my father said. "It's a nice day."

The day wasn't all that nice.

Winter was just breaking up. There were no buds on the trees. There was snow on the ground in the woods. Winter clouds occasionally hid the sun's attempts to warm the day, but the calendar said it was the first day of spring which made it a mental pleasure to be outside and start spring by doing what I loved to do—and what I hoped, like my father, would help me recover my sense of self. "Your voice deepens when you are outdoors. I like you like this. I don't like the sick bit."

"Yeah. It's the only time I'm happy. The outdoors fills my belly, and heals me from the inside out."

"When you sit at a bar, you're a slob. You drool, slur your words, and offend everyone around you."

"There's nothing else to do at night."

"You could read a book in our motel room."

"I'd rather be out on the town. You know that. The alcohol purges my anxiety. By the fifth drink, I forget about Vietnam, the firefight, everything."

"Your life is still just beginning. Dr. Jonas said you must hang in there. Scour your belly with nature. He approves of how you are getting well, but does not like the booze."

"That dam pouring water is churning my guts. For some reason, it reminds me of the MASH unit they choppered me to, after I broke down. The waterfall reminds me I went into an abyss I can't climb back out of the abyss."

"Forget about it. Can't you wash it out of your hair?"

"It plagues me, surrounds me. Engulfs me. I can't run from it—or simply wash it away. Lord knows I'd like to, Dad."

"Your mother is worried about you. She thinks you have let it consume you instead of focusing on the future—better days."

"It's all I think about. That moment, that one fucking moment. They say I'll never forget it. But I don't even remember it. I just remember the firefight, popping off rounds at the VC, then I wasn't there at all. I can't make sense out of anything else in the jungle. Nothing. Not until I was at the MASH unit, in an abyss."

"Time. That's what you need. Time. We'll get it fixed."

Nancy hooked one. "I got one, Jack!" she shouted. "I got one!"

She played the fish in a confused but concentrating way and dragged the northern onto shore. "Jack, would you take the hook out please?" she asked him.

Jack used pliers to extract the hook and Nancy held up her fish for us to see.

"Nice!" I yelled. "But still not a walleye!"

Jack didn't hear my comment, or ignored it.

My father had known both of them when they were married to other people. Now, they weren't married, but Nancy had lived with Jack for years. She was attractive, a good housekeeper, employed at the bank, and loved to do the same things Jack did which were fishing, hunting, and drinking. I liked them both probably because they took their jobs seriously and they were fun to be with. I don't think they ever wasted a weekend.

"Hey, Dave!" Jack yelled. "How come you're not catching any fish?"

"It's because I haven't got a fly rod," my father called back. "My kid's catching all the fish with that stupid fly rod of his."

Dad pulled up the anchor and let the canoe drift down the hole ten yards then dropped the anchor, letting the wet rope slip through his hands.

"There might be more fish here," he said.

The water gushed over the dam and the canoe swayed gently. The river flowed below us between the wooded banks and then around the bend. The day was warming up. I removed my jacket and felt the sun warm my wool shirt. The pool was deep from the pounding water falling over the dam to erode the earth below into a deeper hole. We had dropped our weighted minnows fifteen feet to the bottom and pulled them back up three feet.

I hooked another one, letting the northern pike play a little and released the line as the reel whirred. Then I pulled in. The rod took the weight of the fish. The fish leapt, then dove. I pulled it up, the rod bent double. Dad used the net to land it then tossed the fish on the bottom of the canoe. The fish thrashed against the fiberglass, then lay still, its mouth working.

"Are you men ready for lunch?" Nancy asked.

We pulled up the anchor and paddled to shore and dragged the canoe onto the grass of the campsite. Nancy and Jack had a stringer of five fish.

I started to build a fire, and Jack pulled a cardboard box of food from his pickup and put the box on the table. They had brought vodka and grapefruit juice for Nancy, brandy for Jack, and bratwurst and potato salad for everyone. Jack placed the brats on the grill and Nancy put the paper plates and plastic forks and mustard bottle on the table.

"Nancy?" I asked. "Did you make the potato salad?"

"You bet."

"What a saint," I said.

"You like it?" she asked.

"You bet. It's the best I've ever had."

"Thank you," Nancy replied, noticeably glowing with pride.

Jack was looking in the cardboard box. "Where the hell are the brat buns, Nancy?"

"Oh, God. I probably forgot to bring them."

"You dumb broad," Jack said.

"Jack!" Nancy said.

"Damn women don't know what they're doing," Jack said to Dad.

"I'm sorry I forgot them."

"Brats without buns. Hell."

"Who needs them?" Nancy asked.

"Who needs you?" Jack asked.

"We can eat them without buns," Nancy said, ignoring his rude question, and started arranging the plates. "It's not the most barbaric thing you've ever done."

Jack turned the brats on the grill and then we sat down to eat.

"These brats would be better with buns," Jack said, smiling at Dad.

"Just eat, you guys," Nancy said.

By April 15th, they were married. Although getting married on Tax Day that year didn't make any difference to their returns, Jack still claimed he married her for tax purposes, but I know they were happy with each other—comfortable with each other's banter. They loved each other, and that is more powerful than taxes. I would find out, love is more powerful than a lot of things.

NORTHERN FLIGHT

VICKY'S FATHER WAS NOT in good health, so, though it was planned for her to accompany us, she didn't make the hunting trip. She was also reluctant to leave the dairy in the hands of less experienced co-workers. So I was with my family in my father's pride and joy—a recreational vehicle he had had for less than three months.

Although the summer excursions with my family and Vicky had helped me quite a bit, I had fallen back—relapsed—when the seasons started to change. Progressively, from autumn to winter, I had gotten worse, but the plan was to get me back outside, and with my father's help, I was to help handle tasks in the duck hunting camp, like doing the dishes or cleaning the ducks.

I did not talk much, my speech labored, uncertain, as I fought to make sense. The medical bands the doctor had prescribed to be placed around my forehead and belly restricted my ability to express myself and agonized me—mentally and physically. The only saving grace was to get outdoors.

The trees lining the highway flashed by in a constant roll of green images as the RV made the last turn of the trip to the hunting camp. I was staring out the window, not really paying attention. The most recent dose of antipsychotic drugs had taken over me—over my personality—and I was not really aware or present.

There was, I think, a flock of blue bills flying overhead and angling like little jets above the lake just off the road in front of us. I just hoped they didn't turn around to face me and start quacking, "we sent 'em runnin' Sarge."

We sent 'em running, Sarge, we sent 'em running.

Those words haunted me and could not be shaken out of my consciousness. I felt the anxiety swelling up inside me, took a deep breath, slowly exhaled, and felt the lack of self-control fall back under the weight of the medicine.

The sky was gun metal gray.

The towns we had passed were empty and buttoning up for the winter. The motor home's radio predicted snow and gave the temperature as twenty degrees and dropping. We had three hours before sunset.

"The bluebills are in, gentlemen," my father, who was driving and looking upward through the RV's windshield, said. "When we get to the cabin, we'll load the boat fast and get out to the blind."

The hunt, everyone hoped, would help pull the fury out of me, but even with my fury, I clung to my father, who made sure I was accounted for. We were going to be hunting with shotguns, which raised Dad's level of vigilance.

The doctor's always asked if I ever thought of hurting myself, and I always answered, "no." But I also always wondered who would answer, "yes," if they were really considering it. If I was going to harm myself it would be in a time when the thoughts all flooded in at once. The drugs were meant to keep that from happening, so I didn't dwell on it.

We pulled into the cabin quickly and dressed in long underwear, down vests, sweaters, camouflaged stocking caps, hunting coats, gloves, and hip boots. We carried shell boxes and shotguns down to the boat. White caps whipped the slate-gray lake and waves smashed against the rocks. The wind blew stiffly in the woods.

"With this wind, we'll take it slow along the shore," my brother Tim said, gusts tearing the words from his mouth. "We'll hunt Tamarack Pond."

The dock was coated with ice from the cold waves, and we were careful not to slip. Before lowering the boat, we started the motor to provide traction against the waves. As we pulled away from the dock, icy waves gushed over the transom.

"Bail that out, Mike," my father directed. "We don't want to sink in this weather."

I was bailing out the water when it collected in the back of the boat, and we churned along the shore, the boat pitching and accelerating down the troughs of the waves.

"It's a cold one!" my father yelled in the spray. Ducks flew downwind over the lake like necklaces thrown by the weather.

I reveled in the challenge of five of us in a sixteen-foot boat, pitching and rising in the icy waves that splashed into the interior of the boat and sloshing on the floor. The sense of it augmented—maybe even replaced—the antipsychotic drugs. It was a good feeling sinking back into my psyche. I nodded and smiled, bailing out the potential danger of the water coming in over the transom.

My father, a Navy man, steered the boat expertly, quartering into the waves, and handling the craft in the pitch and yaw of the waves that came over the bow to find good water for the smoothest ride. By the time we reached the camp, our clothes were ice laden, water frozen on our collars, and the earflaps on our caps were soaked. The fire at the camp was ready for us to sit as close as possible and enjoy a roasted meal of duck and potatoes.

Dick and Phil, bachelors who lived in the Twin Cities, business partners of our father, enjoyed duck hunting as much as my family and had arrived at the camp the day before. That was lucky for us, as they had the camp ready. And really lucky for us, as they had that fire and a meal ready for us.

"We didn't know if you were going to make it tonight or tomorrow morning, but it's good to see you," Dick said.

"It's good to be here," my father said. "The roughest part was the boat ride up from the dock. The water's getting rough."

Just a front going through tonight," Phil said. "Should ease back down by morning."

My mother and Tim's wife stayed behind in the camp while, before sunrise, Tim, my father, Dick, Phil, and I got to the blind and pulled the boat into the reeds. The water wasn't as rough as the night before so the decoys placed on the lake wouldn't wash ashore or be lost. So, we threw a few dozen out on the quiet pond behind the blind. Then we loaded our shotguns and prepared for the flight.

It came.

A flock of bluebills angled into the pond with their heads down. They wanted refuge. The wind made their silk-tearing flight silent.

The flock wheeled over the pond and headed for the decoys. They approached low, then settled, breasts up and feet reaching for the water. We fired a volley and two birds dropped. Three bluebills fought for altitude and Phil dropped one over his shoulder as the bird flew toward the lake.

"Leave them where they are," Tim said. "There'll be more."

More bluebills came from the left and cut in. We shot three and reloaded. A single swung along the decoys and flew the gauntlet of our fire. I was last in line and gave the fast-flying bird a lead of a few feet, fired, and dropped it. Then two birds rode the wind high over the blind and going sixty miles an hour. We were reloading as fast as possible, bare hands fumbling in the cold for shells, and the birds still coming. There was no telling where they would enter because they came from everywhere. They flew fast overhead or appeared suddenly over the decoys. There was no point watching them over the big lake. The ducks wanted the quiet of the small pond.

It started to snow. The snow whitened the sky and glanced sharply off the sides of our faces. It accumulated on our shoulders and coated the shore white. It melted on our gun barrels. We could see the ducks twenty-five yards away as they appeared out of the white, driving flakes.

"This is it," Tim said. "We are in the middle of the northern flight."

"They're all over the place!"

Twenty-five bluebills appeared and flew fast toward the far shore of the pond. They vanished in the whiteness. We marked them again when they veered, wings flickering, as they tilted toward the decoys and made a pass.

"Let them work," Tim said.

The flock disappeared again then returned. They were northern blues, big, white breasted, black headed birds, and they wanted in. They swung out over the pond.

"This time."

The flock showed again and set its wings. The birds dipped and swerved for a soft landing. We all fired. Five birds lay on the water. A wounded bird swam and flapped away until Dick killed it, the shot surrounding the duck and the bird lying still, white belly up.

"Let's pick them up," Tim said.

He fought the stiff wind as he paddled the small duck boat around the pond and grabbed the birds. We had fifteen: twelve bluebills, two goldeneyes, and a bufflehead. The ducks lay cold on the seat of the boat. We admired the green tinge in the heads of the bluebills, and the sharp, black-and-white colors of the golden eyes. They were big birds from Canada and snow gathered on their feathers.

Two mallards descended into the decoys. We stood to shoot, and they flared. We dropped one, a big hen. We let it lay in the decoys and a single redhead flew high over us and toward the lake. My father made a long shot and the bird folded and fell into the white caps.

"Let the waves wash it in," Tim said. The bird drifted to shore, and we lined it up with the others in the boat.

Then ten canvasbacks almost knocked our heads off as they flew in off the gale and into the pond. They circled in the slashing snowfall and dropped, with flaps down, toward the decoys. We missed them all.

"That's the worst shooting I ever saw!" Dick exclaimed.

"Man!" Tim yelled and pulled his hat down over his brow. We searched the sky in anticipation of a second chance at canvasbacks which never came.

There was a lull in the shooting, and we had coffee poured from big thermos jugs. Snowflakes melted in the steaming cups then a flock interrupted our coffee break. I spilled my cup as I lunged for my shotgun.

The goldeneyes didn't hesitate. They came gliding through the snowfall with their wings set. I aimed and fired at the lead bird, and it splashed dead in the decoys. The flock flew for the corner of the blind and, when they were high and heading out, Tim shot, and the last bird in line collapsed, falling into the boat right at Tim's feet.

"Well planned, Tim!" our father shouted. "Are you too lazy to drop them in the water?"

We picked up six more bluebills as the cold afternoon passed and, with our limits, motored slowly back to the camp in the dark. Carrying the ducks up from the dock, we heard the lake in the night. We walked through the snow to the cabin.

In the cabin, we slapped the snow from our caps, stripped off our ice-laden clothes, and stoked the fire. We put on clean shirts and pants and mixed the drinks. My father held his glass in the air.

"To the finest hunt we've had in years," he proposed. "To the ducks." We all clicked glasses.

"How did we miss those canvasbacks?"

"Who cares?" Phil said. "That's the best hunting I've ever had."

"We'll get another chance at them again tomorrow."

The northern flight lasted one day, but we had caught it. We had been right in the middle of it. Our hunting weekend had coincided with the frantic, warmth-seeking migration of hundreds of thousands of ducks throughout the state. You get a hunt like that once in a lifetime and you participate in an event seen often by the old-time devoted market hunters and the Native Americans when they shot arrows into a sky black with ducks.

A weekend of that, and I went home a better man, a changed man, filled with nature and the wind on the lake that still blew in my soul.

Now, I could make it through the winter.

AUTHORITIES

S EVERAL ORGANIZATIONS WANTED TO kick us out of the makeshift, homeless camp at Crosby Lake Park. MACV, or Minnesota Assistance Council for Veterans, St. Paul Police Department, St. Paul Parks and Recreation Board, St. Paul Housing Agency, Dorothy Day Center, and my doctors, to name a few, wanted the camp vacated. My parents, who were set on getting me—and Vicky—into decent, warm and respectable housing, were wearing thin on toleration for our life in the camp. The only thing that helped was that I promised them I would continue to see my doctors and continue taking my medicine. Promises I kept for them—and Vicky.

I took ten milligrams a day of Haldol, a powerful antipsychotic, its adverse effect on my sex drive was only counteracted by Vicky's patient persistence. My eyes glazed, shoulders slumped, and I salivated. They called it the "Haldol Shuffle." At first they tried Thorazine, which I could not tolerate, making me catatonic. I stopped taking Haldol for two weeks and thanked God when I went back on it. It quelled my fury and relaxed me as its tranquilizing effect took hold. MACV heard about the camp, but did not know our whereabouts. MACV drove a van in town, rounding up homeless veterans and tossing them in hotel rooms, and then, when it was finally constructed, into the Veterans' Community—a complex of studio apartments for veterans with a community room, TV, and ping pong table, across the street from the veterans' hospital. The woman in charge of the veterans' community gave me a tour, but I preferred the tent camp, outdoors with liquor, which I told her point blank.

The police wanted to arrest us because it was illegal to camp on public land. Kicking us out of the park was their responsibility, and they accepted the duty with vigor. All these agencies begged the police to do something, like dragging us to the joint, and too often the police did just that.

The park board wanted us out of their park, because Crosby Park was not designated for occupancy, only recreation. Responsible for human interaction with the outdoors, the park board felt there had to be an ordinance somewhere in the books that outlawed camping in a city park. They were right—it had been a law since 1865; probably when Civil War veterans needed refuge. So, park rangers patrolled the asphalt path on Cushman carts, supervising people's use of Crosby Lake Park.

St. Paul Public Housing Agency was responsible for housing indigents after they had been through the system. SPHA's apartments were palatial compared to the streets or the tent camp.

Inspections once a year, smoking restricted to twenty-five yards from the building, and booze only in the apartments, were among its drawbacks.

Dorothy Day's mission was to provide food and shelter to people down on their luck, the first rung in the system. After spending a month on a mattress in the shelter before getting an apartment, residents got first rate treatment in a new building and dining room. We avoided Dorothy Day because of theft, and because there was a lack of the kind of comradery we found in the tent camp. Most of the residents at Dorothy Day were down on their luck or bums, riding boxcars from Seattle to Boston.

We almost got caught bringing supplies to the camp. We looked behind us as we walked down the asphalt path and saw two policemen get out of their squad car and shine flashlights along the tree line. We walked along the path, the setting sun casting long shadows through the woods, and found the unnoticeable opening in the forest that led to the camp.

My doctors wanted me out of the camp because of the drinking that went on, and my medication did not mix with booze. I drank on Haldol for years, and the booze potentiated the medication, deadening its effect. Drinking on Haldol set back my treatment, I'm sure. Still, I sat on bar stools and drank myself into oblivion.

That kind of rebellious behavior was prevalent in the camp. And we accepted it as a matter of deviant pride to push back against good advice and authorities. We made friends with a cop—a Vietnam vet who had helped push the Vietnamese forces out of Hue—and he made it a habit to look the other way.

Still, the camp's future was short lived.

SOBRIETY

VICKY AND I MOVED into the high-rise up the street from Crosby Lake Park. Our apartment on the eighteenth floor faced Famous Dave's and Mickey's Diner, the neon lights of which created a pool of glowing warmth at street level we could see when looking down from our living room window.

We faced the airport, too, and saw planes land at night, stacked up in the sky, their blinking lights following the safety of the illuminated runways. The apartment was spacious, the kitchen cabinets, stove, and refrigerator brand new, and the bedroom huge—we luxuriated in our good fortune. I paid the rent and bought groceries. Gas in her car and cigarettes were her business. We were good tenants, enjoying the comfort of indoor living and knowing if we didn't follow the house rules, we would be homeless again in seven days.

Vicky and I even joined Alcoholics Anonymous. We attended meetings at my club and compared notes on our drive home. Vicky did not talk during the meetings. If I talked or told my story, I got something out of the meeting. Vicky listened better than she talked, and that was how she worked on herself. So, I kept my mouth shut and simply watched her individual approach.

She was the wisest woman I knew.

We went to a lot of meetings at the beginning and stayed sober, did not hide bottles, and avoided bars, which, coincidently, limited our recreation. We hung out at coffee shops, with others in A.A., got to know the Fellowship, and actually reveled in being clean.

We found sponsors, worked the Twelve Steps, and discussed them over our dining room table. Both of us enjoyed the meetings and the kinsmanship we were gaining with other members. It felt like a fresh start for both of us separately and as a couple. The world was becoming more clear, and I honestly believed the antipsychotics were having a better, quicker, more positive effect on me without being blocked by the alcohol depressants. We read from the Big Book each night and did a whole lot of growing up in A.A.

We were happy.

Of course, we still had cravings we struggled against, but we withstood the conditioned allure of alcohol. We stayed sober, and I even developed an elaborate spirituality.

We grew into routines, and we eased into old-couple banterings like Jack and Nancy. She kidded that she was leaving me for the next man who came around. I told her I was going to trade her for a puppy. We went on outings cold sober and, if liquor was involved, we simply left and turned in early to avoid the trap of needing social lubricant. We went to supper clubs with friends who drank in front of us, but, as the Big Book stated, if we had a reason to be at an event, it was okay to be there. Getting used to the A.A. regimen, we floundered a little, struggled at times, doubted ourselves at other times, but we stayed sober, became fanatical in the purpose, then settled into the long haul of sobriety, one day at a time.

Neither of us believed A.A. was everything, and we augmented the meetings with every chance to get outside and see an eagle taloning a fish, stare at stars in the sky, or smile at a baby in a stroller. Those experiences were outside A.A.'s umbrella that a lot of people thought covered everything. We knew nature was an escape into a deeper, more spiritual—hopefully, longer lasting—sobriety.

The camp was still operating covertly, but we didn't miss it. Our apartment was a better outfitted little love nest, and we were getting used to the aspects of a more normal existence. Although it was just down the road, we never went back to the camp though I did run into Sam at the VA one day. He had put on thirty pounds—all booze.

Each day, Vicky left the apartment to go to work an hour before I woke up. When she got home, I started dinner, she showered, put on a bathrobe, and stepped into slippers I had given her for Christmas. She sat in our recliner and read the newspaper, while I cooked. I wore an apron, made a wide variety of entrees, and served them with garlic bread—without wine.

We were getting along really well, but then, one night after work, Vicky relapsed with a group of her girlfriends in a bar after work. Undeterred, we redoubled our efforts and she got back on her feet. We celebrated with a meal at our favorite restaurant with iced tea—not Long Island Iced Tea, just, plan old sweet tea. We rejoiced together in each new day, and loved each other more, weathering each struggle and challenge. I doted on her, made sure she had money for gas, made her lunch, and began walking her to the car to kiss her goodbye on her way to work. She felt badly about herself after her relapse, but as weeks passed, the sparkle came back in her eyes, and she smiled.

On our outings into nature, with our emotions exposed to God's earth, we held each other in awe of the world around us. The lakes, fields, and woods were alive with creatures to catch and release, or shoot and take home, and we leapt at the chance to enjoy each event. The outdoors helped heal us, fashioned our relationship, and kept us together, on Mille Lacs Lake, Minnetonka Lake, or Devil's Lake where we kept our limits of walleyes.

The outdoors held Vicky and me together as we discovered our personal truths and sunlight sobered us into a fresh spirituality.

We even started going to church, although the routine and rituals seem to get in our way. "In the beginning was the Word and the Word was God." That is where we started, and together we discovered a brand new Eden.

CRAVINGS

I

"I NEED A DRINK," VICKY said. We were shopping at Aldi next to a liquor store. Vicky also knew J. R. Mac's club was just two bus stops down the street.

"Let's go outside and say the Serenity Prayer seven times."

"Okay. But, I'm hurting."

"Let's leave our shopping cart, tell an employee we'll be right back, and pray for a minute. We can hold hands."

"People will think we are nuts," she said.

"I am nuts. But, it's that or drink," I replied.

We walked through the sliding glass doors, found a quiet corner in front of Aldi, held hands, and said the Serenity Prayer seven times.

"God, grant me the serenity to accept the things I cannot change, the courage to change the things I can, and the wisdom to know the difference."

Vicky had powerful urges to drink and when she begged for a drink, I had the same urges and begged for a drink as well. It was just that I could be more discreet—not voice it. We got through that time, but I knew, and she did too, there would be other times the cravings would win. Maintaining our level of happiness was hard … and painful. Nothing made us think that would change.

We stayed close to each other, enfolding our relationship in our solitude and reliance upon each other.

"You must love that Wilhelm Dairy Farm. You're happy every time you come home from work."

"It's outdoors. We hook up the milking machines at five thirty, the cows give up to five gallons apiece, then we let them graze around, let them be cows."

"It's a mom-and-pop dairy farm, but you love it."

"I tried a nursery first, but they treated us so badly I quit. I hope the Wilhelm Dairy Farm keeps me."

"If you quit, you'd have to look for another outdoors job, maybe not find one and be unemployed, indoors, and broke. You'd be an unhappy person. And I would be unhappy for you."

"It's not a corporate operation. My first week on the job, they had me clean manure. I was so happy to have the job I did not complain."

"You do outdoor things, also."

"I paint the barn and repair the fence. I mow the lawn of the farmhouse. I walk the same path my boss's great, great, grandfather walked herding the cows to pasture."

"I love that you have those feelings," I said.

"I crave that. Those cravings are what ease me away from the other cravings. That is how powerful those cows are. And they could care less," Vicky ended with a smile.

II

But sometimes the cows weren't enough. Or maybe the cravings to go into work were stronger than the cravings to come home to me. Either way. Vicky's friends, once again, talked her into going out with them for a drink after work. She had been sober for five months, and thought one beer wouldn't hurt. It hurt, and she came home drunk.

I met her at the door.

"Vicky, where have you been? You smell like a brewery. Get in the shower and I'll make coffee."

"I just wanted one," Vicky said.

"You're slurring your words. You had a few. Scotch and sodas? Shirley Temples?"

"You son of a bitch! Don't treat me that way. I'm drunk. So *what?* It's a free country." She sat in the love seat, stretched out, but did not put her boots on the fabric.

"Not if you are in A.A."

"It's a free choice. To drink or not." She turned on the TV, and changed the channel to the news. Dan Rather came on, something about Vietnam.

"You chose to drink." I stood in the kitchen, my apron and oven mitts on, with my hands on my hips.

"Yes! And it was *fun*! Do you remember *fun?*""

"How many did you have?"

"What's it to you?" She sat on the loveseat and put her head in her hands, suddenly changing her tone and shaking her head with remorse. "Oh, Mike, I can't do this. I can't do it to you."

"I love you. I'll stick by you. Wasn't that the agreement? If one of us got drunk, the other stayed strong?"

"You keep telling me that, but I'm plastered. I did it deliberately, just to get to you." Outside the window, airplanes stacked up, coming into the airport one mile apart, their lights flashing.

"See that plane out there? First-class passengers are handing over their empty cocktail glasses to the flight attendants. They're coming in for a landing. We can do that. Hand the glasses back to the cravings. Don't let them win."

"No lecture. Please. No lecture."

"Do you need help with your boots?"

"I'll get them off myself." Too drunk, she leaned back on the loveseat and let me pull off her boots. She undressed in the bedroom, and I heard the shower run. "I'll lay out some clean clothes," I told her.

"Don't be nice to me, Mike, I don't deserve it," she mumbled through the pouring water. I picked out a warm sweatshirt and sweatpants from her dresser and laid them on the bed.

"How was work today?"

"A cow gave birth. The calf is beautiful. A new life. Everything went fine."

"Is it standing?"

"Yes, wobbly, but on its feet."

"Were you celebrating when you got drunk?"

"No, Mike, listen to me. I wanted to hurt you."

"I love you. You have to try harder than that. I love you drunk or sober."

She stepped out of the shower wrapped in a towel. With her back to me, she dressed. Then she sat at the dining room table, waiting for me to pour coffee.

"I had fun getting drunk." She watched the black liquid pour into her cup.

"You are starting all over. You have zero days of sobriety. Zero!" I sounded more upset than I meant to sound. Still, I made my fingers in the form of a zero, held them in front of her face.

"It's a number. What a rumba. It's like I never quit. Caught up to me like I was standing still."

"Call your sponsor."

"That idiot? She's got A.A. up to here." She drew a line across her forehead.

"Finish your coffee. You're sleeping this one off."

"I love you when you are angry at me. I'm so loaded."

"Get in bed. I'll sleep in the loveseat."

"You're so nice to me."

"We'll talk about it in the morning."

Vicky undressed, got into bed, pulled up the covers, and turned her back to me.

I turned off the lights, lay down on the loveseat, and pulled a comforter around me. I heard Vicky get out of bed and vomit in the toilet. Then I heard her breathing regularly as she fell fast asleep. I got up to use the toilet, looked at her curled up in bed, and my heart overflowed with love.

Just as much as the outdoors helped me with alcoholism, my love for Vicky helped overpower my mental illness. I took more interest in her life than my own. I wasn't consumed with myself when I was with her. She was a great listener, and I even found personal comfort in watching her listen to me. When she got me to spill my guts to her, her counseling skills were never challenged by my unrelenting talk about my feelings, and my issues seemed to brighten her with a natural calling to help me. In a weird, twisted way, I wanted her to help me because of the joy I saw it cause in her.

I reveled in her company and cherished our time together.

Vicky went back to A.A. with me, the memory of that night fresh in her mind, and the fear it might happen again. With her cravings pushing the limits of her control, we phoned each other once an hour, clinging to our sobriety like a life raft in a whirlpool at sea.

MINNETONKA LAKE

LORD FLETCHER'S, THE SITE of Take-a-Vet Fishing, where I drank to excess in my youth, was an hour's drive from our high-rise. Vicky picked me up with her father, Paul, at six in the morning. She handed me a McDonald's breakfast of a tall stack of pancakes, sausage, scrambled eggs, hash browns, and a biscuit, and I ate it, careful not to spill crumbs in Paul's Volvo. Vicky was beautiful, as she drove through traffic on the freeway, then along the elusive roads that led to Minnetonka Lake and on out to the fishing event that blew the lid off them all.

"Seventy-five of the participants at this event are veterans," I said as we pulled into the parking lot of Lord Fletcher's. "Forty guides are supplying boats, tackle, and bait, and there are fifty volunteers. This lake is the most valuable real estate in Minnesota."

We grabbed a powder sugared donut at a table under the big tent and looked for our guide.

Vicky had to get to the dairy and left, wishing us good luck. Soon after she left, our guide, Ryan, took over. Tall, relaxed, with loose shoulders, and a gentle way about him, he introduced himself and told us the boat was ready. We walked down the dock to his boat, an orange rocket ship that sparkled in the sun, silver flecked, with chrome instrumentation, electric trolling motor, stationary anchor, and 350 horsepower outboard motor. Paul jumped from the dock onto the gray carpeting of the boat.

"That took balls," I told him. He held out his hand and I accepted it, stepping onto the deck of the boat that glistened with brand new shine. Then, he assisted Paul in the same manner.

"Here we go," Ryan smiled. "There aren't any fish in this marina." He untied the boat from the dock, sat in the cockpit and the motor started to rumble. He backed us toward the lake then turned the boat on a dime.

"What makes you contribute your time and livelihood to host veterans?" I asked, as Ryan navigated the marina. He looked over the bow as he spun the steering wheel.

"I want to give back to those who served."

"You didn't serve," Paul asked.

"No, I had a marriage exemption in '64. Then had two children for another exemption after that."

"So, you're not a protester?"

"Well," Ryan said, steadying the boat, "I'm a little too old for that mess. I could have volunteered, but I wasn't going to jump at the chance to go, but the soldiers didn't have much choice."

"I had a choice," I said. "It was the wrong one."

Ryan smiled.

"You're a testimony that it is possible to get through life without the government screwing it up," Paul added.

We passed Chris Crafts in glistening mahogany, yachts in white fiberglass, and sailboats in painted teak, all moored in the marina of Lord Fletcher's.

"I like my job and love my wife and children."

"Are they boys or girls?"

"Two daughters." The motor rumbled the boat along the marina.

"Do you want a son to carry on the family name?" Paul asked, looking at me suggestively.

We passed the exit of the marina, flowered with white lily pads, and headed toward the bay that led to the lake.

"We're not planning any more children." Ryan smiled.

"I was raised with a brother and sister. Our family has kind of fallen apart now," I told him.

"What happened?" Ryan asked, genuinely interested.

"You know. Life. Vietnam, too, I guess," I replied.

"That must be hard to live with. Were you close?"

"Yeah. We were raised pretty close. It just got hard to respark the old times now," I said.

"That's too bad," Ryan said.

"That is bad," Paul added.

"It's the principal fact of my life. I make do without my family around me. But they do the same, I guess."

In the bay, Ryan trolled the motor past another boat coming into the marina then revved the engine as the bow lifted. The motor sounded healthy and hummed as it gained speed.

Paul opened a can of mixed nuts Vicky bought and handed them around.

"Good old Vicky. Always thinking of her men," Paul said.

"She does have a love for others," I added.

The lake was dancing with whitecaps slapping against the hull. Ryan was an expert at anticipating the force of the waves and gunning the engine in response to give us a smooth ride across the windy lake. The boat was wide and long, handled the waves, and hammered the wakes of bigger vessels. Sitting in two of the four pedestal chairs, we withstood the impact of the whitecaps and windswept water.

And the day was shaping up perfectly with a mild temperature climbing, a bright, sunny sky, and a wind that was noticeably laying down into a pleasant breeze. Ryan took us into the middle of the bay, said, "Those houses are as big as hotels," and then navigated the boat through a channel and under a bridge.

We got into a more significant part of the lake, Ryan slowed the boat near a marina of sailboats to reduce our wake, and just beyond that marina, he stopped the engines altogether.

"Let's start here. It's usually pretty good fishing this time of morning," Ryan told us.

We stood in the boat and threw our baits into the wind.

"Nice cast," I told Paul after his line gracefully reached out into the lake.

"Surprised?" he asked me.

"Oh, no. Just impressed," I replied.

"That was a nice cast," Ryan said, turning his attention to me. "These rubber worms are hard to cast. Throw them with the breeze. And be careful not to hook each other with your back casts," Ryan said.

Paul was subject to seizures, so I kept an eye on his balance, but he seemed to be in his element, standing steady despite the gentle rocking.

I have balance issues which I'm ignoring," I said. "I'm able to cast my lure long distances and reel in, without feeling tipsy."

"I've got your PFDs right here," Ryan said, putting personal floatation devices—lifejackets—on the seat of one of the chairs. "No shame in wearing one, but, either way, if you fall overboard, I'll have 'em handy to throw to you."

"Vicky entrusted you to me, Paul. So don't go falling over," I said.

"That water is still a little chilly for me to go swimming today. I'll stay dry," Paul assured me. "Vicky sure does worry though, doesn't she?"

"She looks after you for sure," I said.

"Well. She thinks I'm in good hands with you."

"Do you agree?"

"I think she's right."

Paul and I bent our legs against the roll of the waves. I moved to the front of the boat and leaned against the steering wheel and Paul steadied himself with his left hand on one of the seats. We cast our lures downwind, believing if we cast, we'd catch them.

A little later, we changed locations offshore from a mansion. The house, painted an ungodly shade of purple, with four towers, wings like separate buildings, and countless windows, looked onto the lake.

"We can't all be robbers," Paul said, jerking his head back in a way to let his chin point at the house and indicate what he was talking about.

I said, "The owner might come running out on the lawn and tell us to get the hell out of here."

"I've seen it happen," Ryan said. "Reel in and we can try somewhere else. I don't know why I keep stopping here. I think I just like to show the people in that house what real luxury is."

"I like the way you think," Paul responded.

After we reeled in, Ryan gunned the motor and drove us lickety-split to another bay. And our luck—sporadic for most of the morning—took a turn for the better. I immediately caught a fish. It hit, I felt it tap then tug, and it began to fight as I reeled, the rod jerking and bending with the pull of the fish. The fish came in, I pulled him to the bow, where Ryan stood, and he reached over to draw the fish into the boat. The fish threw the hook and Ryan was left holding an empty line. "I knew I shouldn't have left my net at home."

"Catch and release means I get to catch it first, Ryan!"

Good-naturedly, Ryan nodded.

"How big was it? It felt like a good 7-pounder," I exaggerated.

"Oh, at least," Ryan agreed, knowing it was two pounds at best.

"Paul, it's your turn," I said, and we all focused on catching another fish.

Paul's deep, penetrating eyes gleamed when he got playful. Short in stature, his size belied a big man inside. His skill in electronics supported his family, proud of his job and company. Quiet in social settings, Paul listened to other people, and enjoyed the pleasure of their company, not necessarily what they said.

Like Vicky, Paul thought he was the Lone Ranger and loved Ralph Waldo Emerson's philosophy of individualism. Our philosophies disagreed as I believed in an interconnected world, but he knew Vicky and I had a way of telepathically communicating—a way he appreciated and of which he approved. And, right away, he was kind and welcoming—understanding, perhaps is a better word—toward me when Vicky and I first got involved. He had soon become a second father figure to me.

"The only thing that gives me peace is the outdoors," I told Ryan.

"It gives me peace, too. The only time I am happy is when I'm with my family or outdoors."

"So your job gives you peace?"

"Yes, it does. I have to say I like being a fishing guide more than a hunting guide in the fall, but I miss 'em both in the winter when I am working at the sporting goods shop. That is too slow and too much inside. My family pulls me through the winter months."

"I can understand that," I said.

MARSH LAKE GAME FARM

VICKY WANTED TO GO duck hunting. I explained to her that going duck hunting actually meant shooting at ducks, not hunting them.

"Very funny," she said, squinching her face up into a sarcastic smile.

"Just wanted to make sure," I smiled genuinely back at her. Sobriety—hers and mine—had helped us grow closer and more clear in our communication. We had a deeper understanding highlighted by our natural state of good humor and … well … love. Still I reminded her, "The event does not provide liquor," I said.

"What makes you think I need a drink to shoot a duck? Or to have fun?"

"Again," I explained, "I just wanted to set your expectations."

Her response took on a certain "Vickiness" that I understood as being serious without being overbearing. "I'll be fine." The sunlight promised a hot day as Dick Anderson, the organizer of the event, registered everyone in the bright morning. He reassured us there would be a cooler at the site with bottles of water and soda pop. Meanwhile, as he bantered with us and registered the other hunters, Vicky and I enjoyed the free donuts and coffee.

———————● ●———————

The game manager stood in front of us, wore a tan shooting shirt with a shoulder pad, and held a clipboard. "Who wants to go first and show us what he's got? The only rule is not to shoot anything on the ground."

"I've never shot a shotgun before," Vicky said to no one in particular, but in my general direction.

"Do you have one?" Dick Anderson asked, having heard her.

"No," Vicky replied, looking at me questioningly.

"You can use mine," I reassured her.

"Thanks, Mike. I hadn't even thought about that."

"That's a twelve gauge. Carries a kick," Dick added.

"I can handle it. I'm strong." Vicky said.

"It has never been used by anyone but me, since my grandfather gave it to me when I was sixteen years old."

"I'll be careful with it," Vicky said.

"Shotguns are meant to be fired," Dick said.

In the arena there stood a line of tall oak trees in front of a sequence of five duck blinds, in front of a series of benches, in front of a gun rack, in front of a bit of lake. The ducks flew in, appearing suddenly above the tree line, a thirty-five-yard shot. They weren't passing in flocks, so we picked our birds. The first ducks came through, high, over the trees.

"Mark!" shouted the game manager as the ducks dropped toward the lake. I aimed at the middle duck flying right over my head. At the sound of the volley, the flock dispersed. I pulled on the duck's head as he came at me and dropped him dead with one shot. The bird folded and fell to the ground. A dog retrieved it and took it to the handler behind me. I reloaded, the gun working correctly from the cleaning, and at "Mark! Center!" I pulled on another duck from a flock coming over the middle of the trees, aimed at its head, and killed it with one shot.

"You've done this before!" Vicky shouted from the benches behind me.

I was shooting well. I found confidence that came out of nowhere and shot another duck that folded when I pulled the trigger, felt the recoil on my shoulder, and soaked in the satisfaction I got from the impact of the shot. The duck fell in a clump at the touch of my trigger and the recoil of the gun.

The game manager took me out of the blind when I shot my fourth duck. "Mike! You're done!" he yelled over the blasts of the guns of the other shooters. I walked back to the bench where I watched the others shoot.

I cased my gun at the benches, laid it against the rack, and waited for Vicky to shoot. I showed her how to work the gun, and then the game manager called Vicky to the center blind.

Impressively, Vicky shot four ducks, as I yelled, "Take 'em, Vicky, damn it!" to encourage her. But, she didn't need to be encouraged. She was a natural!

The dogs, a black and a yellow Labrador, chased the ducks in the field from which we shot and brought them flapping in their mouths to the handler, who wrung the ducks' necks and placed them in a pile near the benches. The crippled ducks fell into the field and waddled toward the lake until the dogs got them. Some ducks got airborne again and flew over our heads into the lake as we watched from the benches.

"I don't like this," Vicky said when she was back beside me. "Those poor ducks. I can't believe I shot four of them. They're defenseless against those dogs and shooters."

"We're shooting ducks, not hunting them. Without this game farm, these men might get no shooting for the year."

"Who cleans the ducks?"

"I don't know."

"Isn't there a way of killing the wounded ones besides ringing their necks?"

"It's the most efficient."

"This is disgraceful. And I participated. Let's leave. I don't want to stay for lunch."

"Are you sure?"

"Yes. I'm sure. This is unsportsmanlike. Like shooting ducks in a barrel."

"I don't know what I'm going to tell Dick."

"You better think of something. Here he comes."

Dick approached us in his Stetson and camouflaged shirt. "Is there a problem?"

"Oh, no. I think we just got our first-timers full of a duck shoot," I smiled, knowing he would understand what I was saying.

"Stay and watch. We're almost done," Dick said. "And you did great," he added directly to Vicky. "More get by than we hit. Stay for lunch. It's more unsportsmanlike not to take your four ducks home."

"Okay. I'll stay for lunch."

I nodded and smiled with appreciation for her decision. The shoot had been therapeutic for me. I had taken my daily antipsychotics, and wasn't ready to abandon the prescription, but the fresh air, the comradery, and the feeling of simply being alive that came in its purest form when I was outside had me swollen with an extra layer of joy—an appreciation for life.

…an appreciation for life returning.

THE GROUSE ROAD

WHEN I FIRST GOT back from the Army, on trips with my father to northern Wisconsin, I drank so much that people noticed and remarked about it. My reputation was to sit on a bar stool until I had eight drinks, crawl home to our motel room twenty yards from the bar, throw up, sleep, and do it again the next day.

Then, after living with Vicky and reaching a satisfactory level of sobriety where I was handling my cravings, I went back to go hunting. Well, that was my excuse to my family and to Vicky—who couldn't make the trip because of work. The underlying reason was to show all those townspeople that I was sober and was making great strides in my recovery. It might have been too soon.

●━━━━━━━●

"Is that you, Ben?" my voice asked.

"Fuck you, Sergeant," a voice replied as a face turned around, bloody, distorted, *cracked*. "You brought us here, Sarge," the voice continued. The mouth didn't move as the voice spoke, but an arm slowly raised up with a fist clenched like it was going to hit me in the face, but in slow motion.

"But we got 'em running," my voice replied.

The arm outstretched from a fatigue blouse, turned into a snake—a Bamboo Viper; the one-step-and-you're-dead snake—and waved gently in front of my face. I was frozen with all my energy balled up into an inability to relax. I was absolutely rigid, staring into its eyes.

"Fuck you, Sergeant," the snake said.

The arm dropped, and Ben Gillette's shattered face began to laugh, and his voice repeated, "Fuck you, Sergeant,"

"But I'm well," my voice argued in a conversation that made perfect sense to me. "I can't go back."

Ben's voice laughed louder. "You never left, you son of a bitch. Wake up. You will see. It isn't a dream. This is real."

"No," I whimpered, fighting back tears.

"*Fuck* you, Sergeant." Ben's destroyed face turned into Vicky.

The arm—the snake—the Bamboo Viper—quickly flashed up, and struck her in the neck.

"No!"

It wasn't as often, but I was still waking up at night, sweating from horrible dreams.

———————————● ●———————————

Enjoying the solitude that nature and the open road offered, I drove west of town along the paved, curving, narrow, and dipping drive that passed the cemetery and the small house of the people I knew from the coffee shop. I passed a big hill with maple trees past their peak of color and now red-brown, yellow, and beige. The trees looked like an aged artist's palette.

I took a hard left at the street leading to the greenhouse that was now closed. I drove straight, past houses so small they seemed uninhabitable. I turned right and drove past posted land and down to the dirt pathway leading to where I hunted grouse.

I parked the car on the grass beside the pavement. I got out my shotgun and loaded it. I walked into the woods.

Two days ago, I had noticed that there were no tracks on that road, but as I walked along the path through the woods, I noticed fresh tracks curving through the woods past a small duck pond and between low banks and up to a junction. I followed the tracks across a clear-cut to the right and through another clear-cut on the left and into the woods again. I went through the high grass between the poplar saplings of the bigger clear-cut area.

The tracks stopped, and footprints had gotten out of a vehicle. There was someone up here besides me.

I followed the prints in the dirt and around mud puddles as the path re-entered the woods. It was overgrown and covered with yellow leaves, so the footprints were lost in the accumulated leaves. But it was still beautiful, and, surprising myself, I was kind of glad to know I was tracking someone else into the woods. It was somehow calming.

That's a good sign. I smiled.

I walked up the hill, past a fallen white pine, and reached a ridge of oak and maple above a floor of saplings and yellow and red leaves. Along that ridge I followed an old logging trail, picking up the tracks again. The path fell away and took a sharp left at a swamp of cattails surrounded by jack pines. Brown, withered ferns covered the road. A big rock like the prow of a ship stood alongside the way. The ferns continued. Thorny, red-leafed branches on the boulevard tore at my pants. A big clearing of brown ferns appeared at a bend. A partridge exploded out of the clearing.

Gray and brown, the bird flew straight up, wings whirring like a helicopter, toward a stand of pines. I carried my gun loosely and fumbled to get it up for a shot. The bird made it to the woods before I could aim.

A shot reverberated through the woods, and the bird dropped. A man in a red-and-black wool shirt stood in the road, looked at me for a moment then walked into the woods to find the grouse. The bird flapped in the brush, its wings fluttered furiously, and the man reached down to pick it up. He wrung its neck and put the bird in the backpack of his shooting vest.

"Nice shot!" I called to him.

"I was behind him. I winged him," the man said, twisting the neck of the bird with a quick, sure jerk. The fluttering stopped.

We walked along the passage, and he introduced himself—Lou Johnson.

"Are you the owner of Johnson Hardware?" I asked.

"Yes, I am."

"My name is Mike Reynolds. I am Dave's son."

"I know who you are. I saw you once with your father at Metro's Ski Inn."

"You are a good shot."

"You have to swing with the bird," he said and demonstrated a swing of his gun while he swiveled at his hips.

"I'll try it," I said, and practiced a swing or two with my hips.

"You drink too much," he said.

"No, sir. Not any more."

"You have a reputation in town. I'm glad you are doing something besides sitting on a barstool."

"Yes, sir. I am too. It's been a long road," I said.

We continued walking past a black mud puddle and up a steep hill with small pines and tall grass. I caught the silhouette of a grouse in the grass, aimed at its head, and shot. Then after picking it up, the dead grouse was a warm clump of feathers in my hand, and I put it in my shirt. The tail feathers stuck out between the buttons. I looked around to show Lou Johnson.

But he was gone.

Vanished into thin air.

I looked around to make sure he hadn't fallen, but there was no sound or sight of him. He was gone. It was weird, but I just figured he wanted to hunt alone and had gone back along the pathway. I shrugged his disappearance off, and continued to hunt.

A few minutes later, I heard a gunshot in the distance, and was reassured that he had wanted to hunt alone. And I was glad to hunt alone as well. I had enjoyed our chance meeting, but I was, after all, there for the solace of nature and solitude of mind.

From a hill, the road dipped down through fallen yellow leaves and then up a slow rise. Two partridges broke from beside a tree near a clearing in the path. They were in the open. I shot at one and missed.

The lane continued through more small pines and high grass and up a very steep hill. I was near the end of the drive. On the left was a large park-like wood of old white pines and a few tall, thin poplars with leaves at the top and fallen trees overgrown with grass. A steep ridge formed an amphitheater.

A grouse flew up from behind one of the white pines. It flew through the amphitheater, and I shot and missed. I stepped into the woods. Another bird flew out of the leaves. It swerved through the trees and slanted up into one of the high poplars. I missed that one, too.

I waited. A third bird took off and headed for the ridge. I was unprepared for it and did not shoot. I took another step, and another grouse flew up and headed for the opening in the amphitheater to the left. I aimed and shot, and the bird fell dead.

"Nice shot!" I heard someone call, but when I turned around, thinking Lou had decided to catch up with me, I didn't see anyone.

I put the grouse in my shirt with the other bird.

At the café, I told my story about running into Lou Johnson while grouse hunting. Bunk Knudson and Myron Nelson leaned over their coffee cups and looked down at the counter at me in amazement.

"Who?" Bunk asked.

"Lou Johnson. The owner of Johnson Hardware."

"He hasn't owned that for years," Myron said,

"And besides," Bunk added, "Lou Johnson's been dead for ten years."

"That's right," Myron said, nodding. "His wife caught him in the truck with some woman and took his face off with a 30.30!"

Both men laughed.

A chill ran up my spine and the hair stood up on the back of my neck. I had heard stories like that, but had never been involved with one—or with any supernatural event like that. I was a little scared to walk back to my cabin that night.

●—●

The arm—the snake—the Bamboo Viper—quickly flashed up, and struck her in the neck.

"No!"

"Nice shot," a voice behind me said.

I turned away from the snake with its fangs pumping venom into Vicky's neck and saw Lou Johnson without a face but with remnants of broken teeth grinning through hanging chunks of flesh.

"You got 'em running, Sarge," he sputtered with his jaws wobbling on splintered bone hinges.

It wasn't as often, but I was still waking up at night, sweating from horrible dreams.

MICKEY'S DINER

"**I CAN'T BELIEVE YOU'VE NEVER** been to Mickey's," I said as we walked to Mickey's Diner, three blocks down the street, kicking leaves in the late November weather.

"I'm looking forward to it," Vicky replied. "What should I get?"

"Anything you want, but I recommend the malts," I said.

"A hamburger and a malt?"

"Sounds good."

Early in the evening, the cook and waitress were the only people in the place. I held the door for Vicky and walked her to a booth. We sidled in and grabbed menus off the ketchup rack.

Cinder—who had waited tables at Mickey's since Christ was a Private—came over and asked, "Where have you been?"

"Camping."

"That's no reason to stay a stranger."

"I come back for special occasions, like this one."

"I don't have any heartstrings for you to pluck, but seriously, I've missed you."

"Did Willy die?"

"Yes, two years ago. His son took over."

"Muhammed? How's he?"

"Couldn't be nicer. What have you been up to?"

"Taking care of myself."

"Wait," Vicky said. "Willy was the owner of Mickey's? Now Muhammed?" She looked puzzled. "Then who's Mickey?"

"Nobody knows, Sweetie," Cinder said, looking at me anticipating an introduction.

"Sorry, Cinder, this is Vicky. She's a hired hand on the Wilhelm Dairy Farm. Graduate of Concordia."

"Concordia. Really? How does a graduate of a private school end up on Wilhelm's?"

"I majored in Family Studies. I tried it and hated it. I'm not a doting person. I need the outdoors."

"Where'd you meet this throwback?" Cinder laughed.

"At a homeless camp."

"I'll bet he heated the tent."

"It didn't take much," Vicky said and touched my hand, the first gesture of love besides sex she had shown me.

"So, that's how it is. What will you two have?"

We ordered coffee, a hamburger for Vicky, blueberry pancakes for me, and one chocolate malt for both of us.

"You get around," Vicky said to me after Cinder stepped to the grill to place the order with Bill, the cook.

"This was my hangout for ten years. Especially before I joined the Army."

"You should have kept a good thing going."

"That's why I brought you here." I smiled.

We both paused, looked out the big window then I said, "Tell me about your mother."

"Every day she made breakfast for me and packed my lunch for college."

"My mother took care of me, too, after Vietnam. She did my laundry and made dinner for me every night. I was extremely sick."

"Do you think you are getting better?"

"I don't know. It comes and goes. You help. And getting outside always helps. The outdoors is the most powerful tool I have. Besides you. I think I could get by without the meds by using the outdoors."

"I wouldn't try that. I have heard stories about people who go off their meds. Not pretty."

Cinder laid our plates in front of us. "Do you need anything else? I'll bring the malt when you're done eating."

"This looks great," I said, and we began to eat. "How's the hamburger?"

"There's something about it."

"They grill the bun."

"That's it. It's moist. Those pancakes look good."

I applied butter from tiny paper cups and poured on syrup, as it dripped onto the edges of the plate and the table. I forked into the stack and tasted its blueberries, butter, and syrup. "What prompted you to study families at Concordia?"

"Family Studies," she corrected me. "My father thought it would be a good field to go into to take care of seniors like him. I didn't want to be a nurse."

"And you hated it?"

"Yes. I was terrible at it. I worked as a counselor in a hospital for six months."

"Did you just quit?"

"I had to." She chewed a bite of her hamburger. "The job I have now is a gift of God. Every day I get up in the morning, think of what I need to do for the day, and rejoice."

I cut into a pancake and dipped the bite into the syrup.

"It's a hard job. I'll freeze my ass off in the winter. It was hot in the summer. I've hurt myself twice."

"How's your leg? Has it healed?"

"Enough. I have a big scar where they put the drain. I love those cows so much. They have different personalities."

My plate was clean, Vicky took the last bite of her hamburger, and wiped her lips with a napkin.

Cinder came up to the booth, took our plates, and said, "I'll tell Bill to start that malt. More coffee?"

"Thank you, Cinder. We'll wait for the malt," I said.

Bill came out of the backroom holding an aluminum canister full of vanilla ice cream. He placed it under a mixer that made a racket as it churned the ice cream into a malt. He poured in Hershey's chocolate syrup and let the machine go. Then he poured the mixture into a glass vase and brought it over with the canister. Bill set the malt in front of us and laid two straws in their sleeves alongside.

Vicky and I smiled at each other, withdrew the straws from their sleeves, and inserted them into the malt. We took a sip of the malt, our noses touched, and Vicky leaned back and laughed. "This is so romantic. I can't believe I'm doing this."

"Welcome to Mickey's Diner." We looked at each other above our straws, and the malt drew down in the glass.

Cars sped by on West Seventh Street outside the big window and Cinder and Bill talked behind the counter. The only vehicle in the parking lot was Vicky's. The weather was damp, rain fell all day but now had stopped, and a few drops trickled down the windows.

The malt had subsided to the bottom of the mug where our straws made a sucking noise. We sat back and looked at each other.

I did feel better when I was with Vicky. And there was nothing easier than sharing a malt at Mickey's.

MILLE LACS LAKE

"How are things on the farm?" I asked.

"I got half the barn painted. That's why they gave me the day off for this trip. I repaired the fence, too, all fifty yards of it. They think I am doing a good job."

"You did a good job driving us up here!"

"My father's Volvo is more reliable than my Oldsmobile. If something happened to the Oldsmobile, my credit card could not cover it."

"Do you think it would have made it?"

"I don't know. It may be on its last leg," Vicky said, shaking her head.

"Well, we are here. That is Mille Lacs Lake."

"It's pretty."

"It really is," I said, staring out at the water extending to the horizon. "And there's good fishing, too."

"I'm not much of a fisherman. My father took me fishing once when I was a kid."

"There's nothing to it. Capable Partners put the leech on your hook and set the depth. You just hold the pole."

"I'm looking forward to getting under way," she said.

We carried our gear to the bar and restaurant, where I started with a Diet Coke, and Vicky had a 7Up. Vicky was beautiful with her firm jawline, level, penetrating eyes, and a hint of a smile as she enjoyed being in a crowd of people having fun. She leaned forward over our table to let someone walk behind her chair.

"Tight quarters!" she said, pulling up her chair to let them through.

Hoping I did not drag Vicky up here on a wild goose chase, I asked the manager if I got the day right. She checked the schedule and confirmed Capable Partners had booked the *Pride* launch from four to ten o'clock that night. Vicky and I finished lunch and joined a group of people, some in wheelchairs, waiting to board the big, yellow launch that had a cabin, restroom, walkways with railings, and a captain's tower on a fifty-foot vessel. *Pride* looked old with its pilot house rusted and the paint on the railings chipped, but she was sturdy, built to handle a lot of anglers and withstand high seas.

The dock of timbers extended into the harbor guarded by a jetty of boulders. Speedboats lined the beach, and another dock completed the harbor. *Pride* faced the shore as the afternoon sun beat down on us.

We boarded, I stowed my coat in the cabin, and Vicky set her fishing rod against one of the many supports that held up the roof. "My father gave me this rod."

"It looks like a good one."

"He said it will catch some nice fish."

"That's what you're supposed to do. The rod keeps you from losing them."

People in wheelchairs pushed themselves onto the dock and boarded with a bit of gangplank that lowered them to the boat level since having no rain for a long time had left the lake too low for regular operation.

"Have you signed in?" asked a man holding a clipboard. I chicken scratched my name onto the list of anglers.

"How many are there of us?" I asked.

"About twenty. Do you have five dollars for the captain and five for the biggest fish?"

"All I've got is a fifty."

"We can cash it after everyone's entered."

"I just need $10 back. I will pay for her $20 as well," I said, letting the man know Vicky was with me.

"Great," he replied. "Here, I will need you to sign in as well."

Vicky took the pen and signed the participant sheet. I tucked a ten-dollar bill in my pocket just as our captain, Jake, untied the boat, told us to move to the stern to get the weight off the bow, and gunned the motor, which sounded in good mechanical condition. *Pride* drove slowly away from the dock, the water churned and gurgled at the stern, and Jake negotiated the jetty of rocks that protected the marina. The motor roared as he turned the wheel, and the wide-beamed launch rotated in the confines of the harbor. Sand kicked up as the propeller dug into the bottom of the lake, and Jake revved it, swinging our bow into the waves.

Underway, we headed into the center of the lake, waves slapped the bow, and a brisk wind cooled us. "You're going to freeze to death in that T-shirt when the sun goes down. I'll give you my coat when it gets cooler. I can wear my hoodie."

"I'll be okay."

"Okay. But I have it if you need it."

Pride pranced ahead, and waves dashed from its bow as it plowed into the open waters of Mille Lacs Lake. We could not see the far shore of the inland lake, and waves danced like dolphins, driven by a strong wind.

I thought I would enjoy being on the lake, but my emotions reacted adversely as we motored out.

The wake at the bow threw up spray and splashed my face. The spray from our wake wetted my T-shirt, and I ducked into the cabin when the wash overpowered me. The towering cumulus clouds, expanse of the lake, overarching sky, and intermittent sun drew me out of the situation and placed me squarely in a psychotic episode.

Under my breath, I cursed the lack of efficacy of my medicine. I had taken them as directed, but they were not having any impact. I felt sick.

The rumble of the motors churned my intestines, making them roar with fury. The engines sounded like the incessant whop, whop, whop of Huey helicopters in Vietnam. A reminder of sound combined with the smell of diesel exhaust took me back to the jungle and triggered the memory of the breakdown—or what I had pieced together with remnants of memory, dreams, hallucinations, and imagination.

I saw the grenade exploding in midair. I heard the sounds of the firefight. The smell of diesel was overcome by the smell of burnt carbon. The smell of the lake swirled into the moistness of the jungle. My arms and hands started shaking. I was dizzy. My attempt to steady myself balance on the rail stumbled when I missed and almost fell on the deck before quickly catching myself.

I was panicking—out of control.

"Breathe," I heard a calm voice say. "Breathe deeper, Mike." I heard the voice as it penetrated through my panic and felt Vicky's warm arm pull my weight towards her. "Breathe. Deep."

Reassured by her touch, I followed her orders—her soothing voice surrounding me.

"I've got you," she said. "Breathe."

I inhaled deeply and noticed she was breathing with me. I closed my eyes, and let the dark steady the dizziness of panic. I exhaled, and tucked my chin into my chest. The feelings dissipated and I slowly regained composure.

"You okay?"

I didn't answer.

"Breathe."

I inhaled deeply again—exhaled.

"That's it," Vicky reassured me, still holding me close to her side.

The boat rocked as it lost momentum. The captain had throttled down to a lower speed as we traversed along the surface of the lake.

"Those engines are powerful," I said to Vicky, immediately hearing how much of a thin excuse that was for the attack.

"Do they bother you?"

"I don't know. It was weird. The sound and the smell of exhaust triggered something."

"Are you okay now?"

"Yes. Thanks for being here for me. If you had not held me, I could not have withstood the stress. The motors opened me up like a can of sardines."

"I'm here," Vicky said.

I took one more deep breath, and felt fine. Maybe the meds were slow to kick in, but they seemed to have taken effect.

When we reached the designated fishing spot, I could feel Mille Lacs Lake draw the poison out of me and replace it with my love for the outdoors. I watched Vicky fishing next to me with her special, slight smile of contentment. I knew she was just as happy to be on the launch, fishing—for the first time!—on a beautiful lake. "Mille Lacs is beautiful, isn't it?" I asked her.

"I'm so at peace here."

"The sky goes on forever. We're in the middle of the lake."

"Those clouds are huge. It must be wonderful to live up here." She leaned back and drank in the air. "The air is so clean and fresh."

"We're sober. If we were drunk, we'd be hanging over the rails throwing up."

"I love you for bringing me up here." She put her arm in mine.

"I love seeing it, and being here with you."

Suddenly, someone yelled, "Fish!" and a man's rod on the stern bent double as the fish strained against the line. A racket ensued as Jake ran to the back of the boat, pulled the net off the roof, and leaned over the stern, waiting for the fish to come in. All heads turned to watch Jake land the fish, and a few people ran to the stern.

The man got the fish closer to the boat, Jake landed it, and the man held it for pictures. Jake laid the fish along a board with a measuring stick and announced, "Nineteen inches!"

"Nice fish," I said to Vicky.

"It's our turn," she said.

"Remember, keep your rod tip up when a fish hits."

"I'll hand the rod to you."

"Oh, no you don't. You're landing your own fish."

"I'm such a klutz. I'll probably lose him."

"If you catch it, and it gets away, it'll be your fault, no one else's. You'll have no one else to blame. You're holding that rod, not a committee."

"*Nuts.* I want to blame you." She put her arm in mine, smiled, and leaned on my shoulder. "The philosophy of fishing?"

"Hey," I reminded her, "hang onto that rod."

I reeled in my line, and went over to grab a Diet Coke out of the cooler and brought Vicky a regular Coke.

"I'm so glad you brought me. This is a beautiful day," she said.

"I'm glad you came. There will be a lot of these trips in the future."

"I want to go on all of them. I love you. I just realized it."

"I love you too, Vicky. Very, very much."

"You're down!" Another fisherman yelled at Vicky.

Vicky quickly handed me her Coke can, and began to reel as a unison of voices cried "Fish!"

Jake left the tower, grabbed a net, and ran to Vicky. She had a whopper on her line. Her line quivered with the strain and rod bent double. Vicky reeled, kept her rod tip up, and fought the fish. The fish ran, taking line, then began to come in.

"What do I do?" Vicky squealed.

"Hold onto him, Vicky," I yelled.

"He's so strong."

"Hang onto the rod as you reel. Keep the tip up. That's it. He's coming. Wear him out."

The fish ran, took line, and the reel screamed. Vicky reeled then the fish began to come in.

Jake got the net under the fish and landed him, dragging him onto the deck of the boat, unhooking him, and measuring him. "Twenty-two inches!" Jake yelled, "Biggest so far!"

Someone took a picture of Vicky holding her fish, and Jake threw it back in the water, where it paused, stunned by being out of the water, then swam away, tail twitching, as it dove to be caught again.

"Congratulations, Sweetie," I said.

"He really fought."

"He was a big walleye. You fought him well. I liked the way you played him when you got him up to the launch."

"I didn't play with him. I was trying to hang on to him."

"I'm proud of you. What a great first fish to ever catch in your life."

"Yes!"

"A big walleye."

She sat down next to me, excited over the catch. The waves slowed, and evening was approaching—getting colder. Vicky's bare arms were chilled.

"Please wear my coat. You'll suffer, otherwise."

"If you insist." She smiled from behind her natural stubbornness and put on the coat lined with warm felt. She looked comical, wrapped in the big coat, but still beautiful. She smiled up at me, her arms lost in the sleeves of the coat.

My hoodie warmed me. Still, I was torn between her beauty, her excitement, her love, and the juxtaposed feelings of my earlier panic that came out of nowhere to leave me with a nagging level of doubt. Daylight passed and the mystery of night settled with its own rules.

The lights of cabins on shore of the bay where we fished glowed in the night and the cabin lights illuminated the anglers leaning over the railing. Waves lapped at the hull of *Pride where* the big launch was anchored, motionless in the water.

I thought of Vietnam.

The blank moment of my breakdown lived with me—going over the edge into the abyss, the aftermath of the MEDEVAC, MASH unit, and flight home. My arms locked, shoulders tightened, eyes widened, and I looked to Vicky to steady me.

She put her arm around me.

"Vietnam?" she asked, and I nodded, holding the railing with clenched fists.

"It'll pass." I took deep breaths. Vicky held me closely, I breathed easier, and the thoughts left me.

"Does it help to talk about it?"

"No! Not really. I was just thinking about earlier today. How it came out of nowhere is more worrisome than the actual panic I felt."

"I'm sorry." Vicky held me, rubbed my shoulders, and gripped me closely.

"I'll be okay. Don't be sorry. Be glad you were here. I know I am."

"I wouldn't have missed it for the world," Vicky said.

"I didn't get a bite," I said, shifting my attention back to the fishing. "I'm at the point I'd even take a rock bass."

"You're not supposed to say that." Vicky said. "Think positive. Think about a great, big, fat walleye looking at your worm right now."

"A big, fat walleye?"

"Yes, a big, fat one."

"One fish and you're the *Old Man and the Sea*."

Vicky smiled, leaned against me, and I was happier than I had ever been.

On the way back into the pier, a man from Capable Partners handed Vicky a fifty-dollar bill and a ten for catching the biggest fish.

DEVIL'S LAKE

VICKY HANDLED THE DRIVE to Devil's Lake, and, in the morning, we were on the lake participating in Fishing-with-Vets on Captain Jason's boat. We watched Jason's first mate, Wade, back the boat into the water at the landing near the casino, unhook it from the trailer, and then drive Jason's truck onto the parking lot of the marina before coming back and wading out to get onboard.

It was raining as we pulled away from the rocks of the jetty and navigated the boat towards the far side of the lake. Jason gunned the motor, spraying water up from the transom as rain spattered the windshield below the awning he had put up to keep us dry.

The eighteen-foot aluminum boat banged the waves and skipped across the water as the wind pushed the visor on my cap and forced me to pull it down to my ears. The lake extended to the horizon, and Jason kept the throttle at full speed until a roadway appeared, shored by a bed of rocks, with occasional traffic going by. Jason throttled down the one hundred and fifteen horsepower Yamaha outboard motor, Wade took the helm, and Jason leaped to the foredeck to lower the electric trolling motor.

I glanced over at Vicky, who looked excited at the prospect of catching fish with a guide, on a lake half an hour south of the Canadian border. The rainsuit Jason had loaned her kept her dry, and her hat covered her head. The only thing visible was her smiling face. Her level eyebrows, gleaming eyes, and firm jawline showed in the beige outfit.

She was happy, and I was happy she was happy.

"I'm in a good mood," I said. "Do you have to be on the water to be in a good mood?"

"No. But it helps. The lake soothes me."

They put the trolling motor in anchor mode and began setting our fishing rods in our rod holders on each side of the boat. Jason put worms on our hooks onto rigs he tied the night before, made of a bottom bouncer, slow death hook, spinner blade, and beads. He let out the line from my reel until the bottom bouncer—a two-ounce lead weight— hit bottom, then he reeled up three feet, shut the bail on the reel, and handed the rod to me. I placed it in the rod holder and watched the tip for a strike. Rain pricked the lake, pooled in the folds of my clothing, and dripped from the brim of my hat.

"You've got a fish!" Wade yelled to Vicky, who began to reel. "Keep your rod tip up!"

Jason grabbed the net and moved to the back of the boat.

The fish came in, deep at first, as Vicky's rod bent and jerked, then appeared on the surface as Jason reached for it with the net, then getting the hoop under the fish and lifting it upwards and dropping it out of the net onto the stern of the boat.

"Way to go!" I congratulated Vicky for the first fish.

Jason measured it after extracting the hook—nineteen inches! He slid it into the live well, which kept the fish healthy until we got to shore.

"Keep your rod tip up!" Wade yelled as a fish hit my line. I pulled the rod from the holder and set the hook, reeling, until Jason stuck the net under the walleye that came in thrashing, throwing water, twisting in the net, and wrapping itself up. Jason unwound the fish—seventeen inches!—and we threw it in the live well to join others we caught that day.

Vicky's turn again, she reeled, pulling in another fish, until Jason netted it, then put another worm on her hook, lowering it to the correct depth, three feet above the bottom where fish marked on the fish finder Jason kept on his dashboard.

Vicky kept catching fish, I caught a few more, and Wade let me land his fish in the net as he reeled. Vicky and I daydreamed, and Wade watched our rods.

We trolled the boat in a figure-eight in the area where the rocks bordered the road. As the live well filled with fish, Jason changed our worms, let out our lines, handed the rods to us, and put them in our rod holders to wait for a strike. They both treated us like royalty while Vicky and I fished facing the stern, like ocean fishing, and the awning covered our heads from the rain.

The rain quit, and mild conditions prevailed, with little wind, and smooth water. The sun peered through the clouds, the day brightened, and our clothes began to dry. We ate our bag lunches of ham and cheese sandwiches, Doritos, and Oreos.

Then the weather came in.

"I don't like the looks of that," I said.

It started in the east, low, scudding clouds, beneath a layer of thicker, darker clouds that moved in so fast they made the low clouds tilt in the sky. They looked ominous, so Jason said it was time to head home.

The rain hit as soon as he put her in full throttle.

We drove into it, like heading into a waterfall, and torrents poured onto the windshield, making it impossible to see beyond the bow of the boat. Jason navigated by dead reckoning as water poured from the awning onto his lap. I sat next to him, watching the waterfall of rain in front of us, and staring out the windshield through the sheets of rain. I could not see the shoreline, only water pouring down the windscreen. The rain drenched Wade in the back seat and soaked his coat, while Vicky, having redonned the rainsuit, survived the onslaught.

"Are you staying dry?" Wade asked her.

"Everything but my face." She laughed at the downpour, looked at me with pity, as I got sopped.

The boat banged the waves as we shot across the lake. Jason followed his experience, expertise, and instincts until the shore appeared.

"Great job!" I yelled to him as he slowed to dock his boat so we could disembark. Wade walked to Jason's truck to back the trailer into the water to pull the boat out. Vicky and I walked up the ramp, got into Jason's truck, then Jason jumped behind the wheel to drive us to the resort.

Another day fishing on a lake took my anxiety out of me, threw off any feelings—or potential feelings—of despair, and gave me a routine to rely on. Fishing-with-Vets made it even better as the organizers took care of us, cleaned our fish, fed us, and provided a hotel room with a shower. Vicky and I slept together in one of the twin beds in our room. A day on the lake, the rainstorm, and dinner made us eager for each other. We made love, fell asleep, woke to each other in the middle of the night, held each other, and made love again, sleeping until morning.

"Last night wasn't bad for a man who can't catch as many fish as I can," she taunted, getting up to take a shower.

"The northern air brought it out in me."

"You didn't miss a beat."

"We're sexually compatible, anyway. Who cares if we don't get along otherwise. Remember the first time we had sex?"

"At the camp?"

"I never told you that you were the girl for me."

"I wanted it to last forever."

"I want us to last forever," I said.

Vicky, smiling, leaned back to look at me from the bathroom doorway.

ORDWAY PARK

VICKY CALLED FROM THE Wilhelm Dairy Farm, said she'd be home late, and to take my time with having dinner ready. The fence she repaired had broken again and the entire herd had gotten loose, running free all over the countryside. Her boss had asked her to stay late and help round up the cows. I told her I'd wait for her for dinner and that the spaghetti would keep.

That afternoon, after she had called, I took a walk down to Big Louie's, a restaurant in lower St. Paul where I sat at the bar and sipped Diet Coke. As I walked out the door on my way back to the apartment, I heard music coming from the park. A band was playing an early evening concert, and people lined the walkway, sat on boulders, park benches, or in collapsible, blue chairs. I was drawn to the pounding of drums and the clinking of a piano, so I walked over.

Sitting on the bricks right in front of the bandshell, I was only a few yards away from the band. There were rows of blue lawn chairs reserved for employees of the credit union that had sponsored the concert, and to my left was a group of young people, sitting or sprawling on the brickwork. The park was surrounded by apartment buildings, restaurants, and the Union Depot, its lights illuminating an already lit up amphitheater.

A young man with an unruly Afro and a young woman with a short black dress and combat boots played music I could not identify in terms of genre. It had the soaring lilt of energetic mood music. The beat was powerful. The duo sang joyously, throwing back their heads, and simply having fun as the man banged on the electric piano and the girl struck the electric drums with flying drumsticks. Another girl, with an operatic voice, joined them. Their voices soared through the downtown neighborhood.

Children played around us, chased a soccer ball, or danced to the beat. A homeless man, in a dirty, white T-shirt jitterbugged with a homeless woman who threw punches at the air. Another pretty girl with long legs in tight blue jeans, with a cut off T-shirt revealing her belly, sat on the brickwork next to an overweight young man and a woman wearing paisley tights.

An older man tapped my shoulder and offered me a chair next to him. I thanked him and sat down in a lawn chair, more comfortable than brickwork. The name of the credit union appeared on a piece of paper on the seat of each one. People in chairs listened to the music in comfort.

People danced, took pictures, walked around the park, or watched their children, dancing in a circle or listening to the band as their parents held them in check. The sound of the band reverberated through the park, amplified by huge speakers and a sound system operated by a man under a tent behind me that canopied the control panel. A man with a taco he had gotten from a vendor in the park sat down next to me as I listened to the band. A thought—one of those random guerilla foot soldiers that all too often snuck up on me—made me think of my life before my breakdown. I was always out at night and valued that experience as much as what I did during the day, whether I was in the Army, going to college, or holding down a job. It didn't matter—at quitting time, I headed for town.

Being around other people had been important to my personal growth. Now, even in that downtown crowd of people out and enjoying the music, I was alone. It was a situation one of my doctors had emphatically told me to avoid, yet, there I was, feeling isolated and distant. And it struck me that I had no social life of my own, no outlet, and no life really worth living. I lived each day, knowing I would never make up for what I lost—the fun, the rock concerts, the parties, or the social life. I sat in the chair and listened to the band, as these thoughts filled my mind, amplified by the speakers, driving the sounds and scenes into my brain.

I felt alone. Frightened. Angry. I felt anger toward God.

The thought of what I was going through saturated my presence until I wasn't present there at all. I was exiled into the scene as an object with no subjectivity left. I was … lost.

I don't remember doing it, but I walked to the bus stop, taking the bus home, but unaware of the passengers and without being mindful of anything—no emotion, no thoughts, no concept of time.

But I made it, got off at the right stop, and walked to the high-rise. I took the old elevator to our apartment, opened the door and floated in on a total lack of corporeal substance. Vicky was still at work.

Yes, still at work, I remembered. *Loose cows.*

I took a dose of medication—an extra dose, earlier than prescribed—and went to bed.

Loose cows. We got 'em runnin'.

I went to sleep—no … I passed out.

"Are you hungry?"

I heard Vicky's voice, but it was filtered through sleep and distance.

"Mike?"

I woke up—no … I came to.

"There you are," Vicky was saying though the sound was weighed heavy by the haze between us.

"Hey," I said, pained to push out the one syllable.

"I tried to resurrect you early when I first got home. Are you okay?"

"Yes. I think so," I said, trying to put a puzzle together. *What happened?*

"I went out for some burgers and fries. You didn't make spaghetti."

"No. There was music."

"Music?"

"I went to Big Louie's. The park. What time is it?"

"Hmmm, nine-thirty," Vicky said.

"Wow. Are we at home?"

"Yes. Mike, what's wrong."

"I must have blacked out."

"Were you drinking?"

"No," I reassured her as I was slowly gaining awareness.

She leaned forward towards my breath; kissed me to cover up her suspicions of how she thought it would smell. "That's good," she said.

"I wasn't drinking," I said. "It was worse. I was alone."

RELAPSE

I **GOT A JOB OFFER** I thought would work out as a cashier at Walgreens. I had not held a job since leaving the Army, but this one showed promise. I thought it could even be a long term employment allowing me to move up into the management ranks.

To celebrate the offer I decided to have a drink. Vicky was at work, and my rationale kicked in to approve the idea without much thought. I was consistently plagued by cravings, and it had been a while since our last trip to hunt or fish. The next trip was still 10 days away, and I caved. *One drink. What could that hurt? I had a job!*

I had five years of sobriety.

I took the bus toward downtown, excited and scared. I felt like I was going to basic training in the Army. I had decided on Shamrock's, but the bus stopped at J. R. Mac's for another passenger, and I got off. It looked like a friendly place, and Shamrock's—as I remembered it—was a hell hole. I opened the door of J. R. Mac's and walked in.

Forgetting it was early in the day, I expected J. R. Mac's to be crowded with people, but there were only a few people in the corner, next to a pull tab booth—the bartender was picking up salt and pepper shakers. He wore an argyle sweater tucked into old blue jeans.

I took off my coat, placed it on the back of the bar seat, and sat down. I felt at home. The bar was dark and neon signs glowed within it.

I ordered a Manhattan. I told the bartender I wanted cheap bourbon, with bitters, cherry juice, and a cherry.

"What kind of vermouth do you want?" he asked.

"Sweet," I said.

He looked under the bar and found a bottle of sweet vermouth.

"What kind of bourbon are you using?" I asked.

"Makers Mark or Jim Beam," he said, to give me a choice.

"Which is cheaper?"

"Jim Beam."

"Use Jim Beam, please."

He made the drink.

I wore my five-year Alcoholics Anonymous medallion on a chain around my neck. I considered taking it off and placing it on the bar. I considered telling him about it.

He placed the drink in front of me and I laid a ten-dollar bill on the bar. He gave me change, but I left it on the bar. The drink cost two dollars and a half. When I had been drinking heavily, at dives, they cost one and half bucks. J. R. Mac's was a neighborhood bar, not upscale.

I sipped the drink. The alcohol burned my tongue, scalded my throat, and warmed me. I could taste the bourbon, sweet vermouth, and cherry juice. The drink was delicious. I was not used to the burning sensation, but I liked it.

There was a baseball game on the television over the bar. The Giants were playing somebody. I loved to watch baseball and watched the athleticism of the players. The players were young, in wonderful physical condition, who made plays hard to believe.

I sipped the drink. The bartender moved around behind the bar and the people behind me talked softly. It was a quiet, weekday afternoon.

I began to feel the effects of the booze. I was getting happy, emotionally full, and my imagination began to soar. I nursed the drink.

Then I slid it out from me and in front of the bartender. "Do you want another one?" he asked.

"Yes, please," I said.

"Same way?"

"Same way."

He made the drink, put it in front of me, and withdrew two dollars and fifty cents from the money I had on the bar. He slid it away from me with a flourish.

"Thank you," I said. I had not forgotten how to drink at a bar and was making a Chinese tea ceremony out of it.

The second drink got me drunk. I continued to watch the game. I began commenting on it. "Don't swing on that pitch," I said, or "They got him!" as they threw a man out at first.

I sipped the drink, noticing only the burning alcohol, the taste of the Jim Beam, and the sweetness of the drink.

It was a good Manhattan.

———————• •———————

I thought about myself for a while at my daily devotions. I had no consequences from the night before, except a slight hangover. I had a headache. I hadn't lost my family, driver's license, or job.

I told Vicky what happened, and she did not bat an eye. She had been there. She understood. That's what my morning-after justification tried to convince me. And I told myself I had no remorse.

But that wasn't true. I was eaten up with remorse.

I had friends who depended on my sobriety, but I resolved not to tell them. Nor would I tell my brother, whose reaction would've been predictable. He was an A.A. Nazi and devoted to its principals. I made a mental list of people to tell, and people not to tell.

I thought about a woman I had met once at an A.A. convention who had relapsed after thirty years of sobriety. She had showed up at a restaurant, where she was a waitress, drunk. She had laughed about it.

Then I contemplated my spirituality. A.A. was a spiritual program because alcoholism was a disease of the soul. That's why they called booze, spirits. I repeated to myself that I did not feel guilty—would not feel guilty. But I did feel guilty. I had worn my sobriety on my sleeve like a gold cufflink. Now it was gone. I had less than a day of sobriety.

I needed to go to an A.A. meeting and confess. I needed a psychologist. Instead, I went to a coffee shop.

My inner peace and serenity were gone. I was tormented and bewildered, lacking any feeling of the joy I had been exporting lately. To the young girl who brought coffee to my table, I was another drunk buying a redemption.

I waited for the consequences to hit. At one A.A. club, I watched as its members pilloried a man who relapsed. I hoped it would not happen to me.

My belly, where my feelings of joy had resided, was dead. My face, once filled with beatitude, was barren.

I had fallen off the wagon.

PELICAN LAKE

MY BROTHER, TIM, PICKED me up at three thirty in the morning. Hungover, I met him at the door and tried not to show it. His dog, Maddie, was in her cage in the back of his 1966 International crew cab truck. I dragged my duffel bag of hunting clothes, shell box, and thermos to his car and threw them in the back seat alongside my shotgun. I wore long underwear, a hunting cap, and a camouflaged fleeced shirt. We stopped at the Super America gas station, and I filled my thermos with fresh coffee.

I had spent the night in the bar, and had gone home after eight Manhattans, just like the old days before Vicky and I quit together. It was like my days in the tent camp, when I drank to pass out—except Vicky was not there. She was disappointed in my relapse, and could not be coaxed into joining me. I should have admired her strength, but was too wrapped up in my desire to drink. Now, my breath smelled, my eyes were glazed over, and my tongue was thick in my dry mouth.

My brother, despite being angry that I was so impaired, demanded that we still go on the scheduled hunt at Pelican Lake. He pulled out of the driveway of my high-rise and headed north—about an hour from Minneapolis. We talked on the way up the dark freeway, lit only by the dashboard glow.

"How are you?" he asked.

"I'm tired all the time," I replied. "I'm suffering from fatigue."

"What's causing it?"

"The VA is not sure," I said. "It could be my abuse of alcohol."

"Lay off that stuff," Tim replied. "It will sap your strength. How much of it do you drink?"

"Eight Manhattans a night."

"Ouch," he said. "That's way too much."

"It could be a lack of handball or not enough sleep, too," I stated, trying to justify—and deflect—my relapse. "We're starting with the booze."

"Will you be alright on this trip?"

"I'll be fine."

"I hope so."

"How are your kids?" I inquired.

"They're fine," he replied. "Ben is playing soccer. He's got our family's legs."

"How's Kari?"

"I'm going to hunt with Kari at the cabin this weekend."

"You taught her a love of the sport."

"Are you and Vicky still an item?" He knew I had a habit of losing women for one reason or another.

"Yes. Very much so."

"How does she like working on Wilhelm Dairy Farm?"

"She loves it. She milks the cows in a shed, but otherwise she's outdoors. That's all she cares about."

We drove through the tunnel under Minneapolis, past the Basilica, and north, past shopping outlets, oases of gas stations, and past two police cars by the side of the road with their lights revolving.

"They got him," Tim said. "Two of them means he was going fast."

"They were talking to him," I observed.

"They go like banshees these days," he said, verbalizing his disapproval of speeders disregarding the 55 mile an hour speed limit.

"Poor man," I sympathized. "They'll write him up."

"He deserves it. Pour me another cup of coffee."

"I told you to get the large cup," I said, taking his cup from him, taking the lid off and refilling it with coffee from my thermos. "Here," I said, handing it back to him.

"Thank you," he said. He turned off the freeway, toward a gas station, where we pulled in, used the restroom, and Tim stopped in front of the granola bars.

"How many granola bars did you bring?" he asked.

"Six," I said. "Two from last year and the four I bought this morning."

"I'm sure last year's bars are *wonderful*," he stated.

"I ate one on our last trip and did not croak."

"Not yet. I'll go ahead and buy some more. Whoever invented these things is a genius."

"I don't know. I kind of like Pop Tarts better," I replied.

"You were always the weird child," he said.

I refilled my thermos and Tim bought a large cup. He paid, and we got back on the road. We drove along county roads, past mailboxes in the dark, turned a few times, and came to an obscure dirt road where we entered the public access of Pelican Lake. Four cars with trailers were parked to one side.

A man was launching his boat next to a dock.

"That's Gary Nicholson," Tim said. "He'll get a good spot."

We stopped the car, got out, and Tim set up his boat on the trailer. I dressed in my Columbia Quad of insulated pants and coat, and pulled on my hip boots.

Tim backed the trailer down into the water, and I released it to let it float into the lake. When it was clear of the trailer, Tim pulled the truck up into the parking lot and walked down with Maddie on a leash to where I had the boat secured ready for us to get in it and get underway. A sudden chill reminded me I had left my fleece shirt in the truck.

"*Dammit,*" I said.

"What's the problem?" Tim asked, hoisting Maddie into the boat.

"I forgot my shirt," I said. "We're going to be sitting around and I want to be warm."

"Here's the keys. Hurry up," he ordered. "And remember to lock the truck back up. I don't want anyone stealing that beast." Tim was dressed, the boat was ready, and our gear was in it.

"I know you didn't fill up the gas can, so I'll meet you at the dock," I said over my shoulder as I headed up to the truck.

Finally dressed, I walked to the dock, and Tim pulled the boat around and backed it into the water at the boat ramp. I guided him. He stepped out of the car and, together, we launched the boat, sliding it off the trailer, into the water. It went in with a splash. I held its rope and stood on the dock while he parked the car and trailer and uncaged the dog. The little bay was quiet. I held our boat by the rope and watched other hunters put in their boats.

Walking back down the ramp, he held Maddie by her leash and put her in the boat. He got in then I stepped into it, careful to avoid bags of decoys, my shotgun, which was on a seat, my shell box, and thermos which were on the floor to one side.

The dock worker came out to the gas pump and filled our gas can. "A dollar-fifty," he said.

"I knew it was empty," I said to Tim.

Tim smiled, handing over two dollars. "It's good now. Go ahead and sit in the bow."

The dock worker put the two dollars in his pockets and pulled out two quarters. "Thanks, guys. Have a good day out there."

"Thank you," Tim said, and pushed away from the dock. Before he started the engine, he wanted to test the spotlight, but he accidently dropped it in the water. It was tethered to a line, so he could pull it back out of the water, but upon trying the switch, it didn't come on.

"Do you have another one?"

"Yes," he said, angry. He rummaged in his duffel bag and pulled out another spotlight.

"It might work when it dries out," I said.

"Yeah, maybe," he said, "But at least I brought this one. I hate hunting without a light."

He started the motor and drove us through an isthmus of reeds and into the big lake. I held the dog by her collar, and she sniffed the wind. The stars were fading as the sun paled the sky.

—• •—

On the lake, I watched for deadheads in the water. We passed an island of woods, which was a dark silhouetted streak in the early morning, and lines of darkness I knew were reeds. Flocks of coots flew alongside us, their feet pattering the water.

"Northwest wind," Tim said over the purr of the motor.

"Do you know where to set up?" I asked. He nodded his head in assurance.

We drove to the west end of the big lake then stopped at a bed of reeds.

"I know where we are," I remembered. "We hunted here before."

"Last year, when we had that good hunt," Tim said.

The lights of other boats moved across the lake and the lights of hunters already in their blinds shone across the bay.

"That man is not too close," Tim observed. "There's no one around us."

"When can we lay decoys?"

"Let's do it now," Tim said, and threw the anchor, tied it to a strut on the boat, overboard.

"We'll start with the baldpates," he suggested. "They're on the floor. You can pull out the mallards too."

I lifted the big bag of mallard decoys from the bow and placed it on the floor of the boat in front of me. Tim pulled in the anchor, which came in without effort. It was an empty rope in the water.

"I lost my anchor!" he exclaimed. "I'm not having a good day."

"Do you have another one?"

"In the bow, under the mats," he said. "Hand it to me."

I reached under the grass mats, found a big two-pronged anchor, and handed it back to him. "Tie it good," I said. "What did Dad used to say? 'If you can't tie a knot, tie a lot.'"

He tied the rope of the anchor to the strut, threw it in, and we began laying decoys.

"Unwrap them and hand them to me," he ordered. He forced me to work quickly as an antidote to my dragging movements—the coffee had helped a little, but not much. I felt myself moving against his orders and my heavy inertia.

"I'm trying to help you," he said, as I unwrapped the decoys, handed them to him, and he threw them, placing them in the water.

"I know you are," I said. Soon we had a flock of twenty mallard decoys bobbing in the little waves in the water.

"Divers downwind," he said, and lifted the anchor and let us drift. "They're in the big black bag."

I lifted the bag from the bow, placed it between my legs, and opened its drawstring. I took out a bluebill decoy, unwrapped it, and handed it to him. He stood in the stern, while I sat in the bow. I struggled to keep up.

I unwrapped the lead weight that was wound around each decoy's head and unwound their strings which were in figure eights around their bodies. I handed each decoy to Tim who threw them in as fast as I could unwind them. Then twenty bluebill decoys lay bobbing in the water. I finally felt my strength returning.

Tim stood like a gondolier and pushed us into the reeds. The big boat slid into the rushes that brushed the sides of the boat as we went deeper into their cover. "This looks good," Tim decided, and threw in the anchor.

We set up the blind. He designed it, and, with two pulls of bungee straps on each side, I pulled it erect and hooked the bungee straps to the bow. We arranged the netting on its sides then placed panels of grass mats over the motor and the bow. We were blinded in. Tim sat down, I poured him another cup of coffee from my thermos, and I ate a granola bar.

"I should have gotten a Pop Tart," I said.

"These are better for you," Tim said, opening up his own granola bar.

"My goal today is to shoot safely," I informed him.

"I never hunted with someone who said that," Tim said. "What does that mean?"

"I'm tired," I explained. "I want to handle my gun safely."

"It's not being tired you are suffering from," he returned.

We watched the sky lighten. According to the chart in the rule book, it was shooting time. I was surprised it was legal to shoot that early. As bright as the sky was getting, the decoys were black figures on the water.

"Is your gun loaded?" I asked, after a while.

"Yes," he replied.

"I'll load mine too." I shoved a shotgun shell into the chamber, which clanked shut, and shoved two shells into the magazine. It was an old gun, fitted and given to me by my grandfather when I was sixteen years old. It was heavy, but it worked, if I kept it clean and oiled.

"You can straddle that seat," Tim suggested. I turned in the rotating seat, straddled it, and peered over the edge of the blind.

"I've got a great view of the mallard decoys," I said.

"Good."

"The line of the decoys is pointed upwind," I said. "Good set up."

A few shots echoed in the gray morning light.

"Can we shoot?"

"Not yet," Tim said, always conservative. "Too dark to see what we're doing."

The shadow of a duck passed over the decoys in front. A few shots reverberated from the north shore, where two parties had put in in the night. The sky lightened, and the wind picked up.

"That wind is giving the decoys a little motion," Tim noticed. "We can shoot now. If a duck comes in, take it. No goldeneyes or buffleheads."

We watched the sky and a few other hunters shot on occasion. Then a flock of ducks appeared in front of Tim who did not see them. Immediately, they began to land in the decoys.

As one set its wings to come in, I shot at it. I was behind the bird, and it accelerated to escape. I caught up with it with my gun barrel and shot it dead with the second shot.

"Good shot!" Tim exclaimed. "Bufflehead."

"I'll take it," I said. "I've been skunked too many times, and anything is good."

Tim unhooked Maddie's leash and yelled "Fetch, Maddie!"

Maddie leaped from the boat and began swimming toward the duck. It was thirty yards out. She grabbed it softly in her jaws and brought it back. Tim pulled her dripping onto the dog ladder he had built, took the duck from her mouth, and handed it to me. Maddie shook herself off, and I admired my duck.

It was a hen bufflehead, small but a duck nevertheless. Its brown head had a white streak. I placed it between my legs on the seat.

"You got a duck!" Tim stated.

"I'm surprised you did not see them," I said.

"They come out of nowhere."

"It's that kind of day," I noted. "We have to stay on the ball all the time." My fatigue was fading.

The edge of the eastern shore across the bay began to glow. "We're going to have the sun in our eyes," Tim said. "You'll lose that pale look."

"That's from my nightlife," I replied.

"You need to lose *that*, too," Tim said.

We marked ducks in the air all morning. Strings of ducks flew over the far island, like little necklaces, and Vs of divers flew high above the lake on their way south, flew along it, then lifted to head south.

"This is the way it is on Pelican Lake," Tim explained. "They come in, give us a roll then fly out."

The eastern shore glowed like a caldron and the sun rose. Its glare was in our eyes. The air got cooler as it always did at sunrise. There were wisps of stratus clouds in the clear sky.

I stood up to urinate into the lake, and almost fell over. I grabbed the fragile blind to keep from going into the water.

"Are you okay?" he asked. "That's a loaded shotgun in your blind."

"I'm sorry," I replied. "I was stiff from sitting so long."

"You're moving like an old man."

"Not enough handball," I suggested.

"I lost an anchor already. I don't need to lose a brother on the same day," Tim said.

I urinated into the lake and returned to scanning the sky. Then a flock of big ducks appeared over the decoys in front of Tim. There were twenty of them, against the brightening sky. They flared and their white bellies showed. We aimed in on them and fired.

"Did you get one?" I asked, after they were gone.

"Yes," he said. "Maddie, Fetch!"

The dog leaped into the water, swam toward Tim's bird, and brought it in. She chugged as she swam. Tim pulled her onto the dog ladder and exclaimed, "Look at this!" He held up a huge duck with a black, iridescent, green head and blue bill.

"It's a bluebill!" I shouted. "A drake!"

"That's what it is!"

"I aimed at the bird below yours, but was behind it," I said.

"We're going to have a shoot!" Tim shouted, excited over his kill.

The morning proceeded. We continued to mark ducks. There were many shots from the blinds in the north.

"Mark," we declared periodically, as we tracked ducks that flew low along the water, or high overhead.

A flock approached us from the south, we saw them coming, and they flared when I brought my gun up too soon to shoot. A hen mallard flew along the outside of the decoys. I aimed at it but did not shoot, afraid of crippling it with a long shot. Three birds flared off our stern, but Tim called me off the shot.

"Too long," he advised.

"I want them coming in with a sign around their necks that says, 'Shoot me,'" I joked.

"I like them with their wings set, too."

Then a flock of canvasbacks roared right over us.

"Good Lord!" I exclaimed. "They sounded like jets!"

"Let's see if they come back." We watched the flock fade into the bay, but they did not return. A flock of bluebills appeared suddenly, and we saw them when they were in front of me, over the mallard decoys, too late for a shot.

"Bad mark, Tim," I chided. He never saw them coming. They were big birds, as close to us as the flock from which Tim dropped his bird. We marked ducks that flew in to get it from the hunters in the north and flocks that did not give the lake a second look, but flew high and going south.

"I've got the wind in my face, but I'm warm as toast," I bragged.

"That Columbia Quad was the best thing you ever bought," Tim stated.

"The wind is picking up. Feel it?" I asked.

"It's shifted," Tim noticed. "The weatherman was wrong. He said five to ten miles an hour."

"This is over fifteen miles an hour." There were whitecaps on the lake and the wind was from the north instead of slightly behind us, as it was in the morning.

"I wish this wind was more at our backs," Tim said. "It is not right for this blind." Tim laid our rig and chose our blind for a northwest wind.

"It's slow," I said. The sky was empty, and we were not marking ducks. The sun was high. The wind was in my face, and I began to shiver.

"Let's give it another half hour," Tim said.

After forty-five minutes of seeing ducks fly up the lake, flash white as they changed course, then disappear into the glare of the sun, Tim said, "It's eleven fifteen. Time to pull."

Almost crying from saying goodbye to the outdoors, I acquiesced.

We pulled into the driveway of the high-rise and people sat in the sun on the benches by the front door. I got out, pulled my bag, shotgun, shell box, thermos, and bag of ducks from the car.

"There must be a whole deer in that bag," Vicky smiled. I smiled back at her, and she knew the day on the lake was what I needed. All was forgiven—not yet forgotten—but forgiven.

A CHILD

VICKY CALLED FROM WILHELM Dairy Farm and asked to meet me at our coffee shop, Dunn Brothers, two bus rides away. I did not ask what the meeting was about—I only knew it was important. A light rain was drizzling from low clouds that moved into town blocking the sun that had regaled us for several days. The weatherman predicted it would keep up all day. Still, I had not dressed for the weather. The gloom of the day had settled in and rain drenched my clothes and my spirit. When the bus arrived, I boarded with my service-connected ID, and sat down on the front seats reserved for seniors and disabled people. I pulled the cord and the bus stopped at Grand Avenue, the most expensive street in town. I got off the bus, and walked to the next bus stop, where I waited fifteen minutes, as people in Audis, Mercedes, and Cadillacs drove by.

The bus showed, I boarded, and sat down next to a woman with a brown paper grocery bag. I got off at Snelling, walked back half a block to the coffee shop, where I met Vicky at a corner table. She looked sad, miserable, her eyes red, mouth wet and downturned, and shoulders stooped. She wore a T-shirt, wet at the shoulders. A panoramic photograph of St. Paul hung on the wall above her.

"What's up?" I asked, pulling up a chair, thinking Vicky's appearance could not match anything so cataclysmic.

She looked away.

"Tell me," I said.

She looked at me, looked away, and took a deep breath. Gaining strength from an invisible source, she looked at me again, and said, "I'm pregnant."

"I thought you were on the pill."

"It's not one-hundred percent effective."

"How did you find out?"

"I just came from the doctor."

"I'm overjoyed. Why the sad look?"

Her strength faded. She looked away and I watched her wipe her eyes with a cloth napkin from the table.

"Can I get you anything?" a waitress asked, seeming to appear out of nowhere.

I shifted my attention towards her, noticing Vicky already had a cup of coffee in front of her. "Yes, just a cup of coffee," I answered.

"You got it."

"Vicky?" I refocused on her as I waited for a response.

"You may not be the father."

"You're kidding me?"

"No. When you had relapsed," she hesitated, "I did too."

"What do you mean?"

"I was with my girlfriends. Just for a couple of nights. When you were out."

My feelings weren't sure how to respond. I was angry at her for what she was saying, but I had enough residual guilt to know if I had been there, she would have gone out with her girlfriends. Then, compounding those feelings, I felt new guilt for blaming her.

"Okay…?"

"and," Vicky inhaled and looked at me despite her chin quivering, "I was with someone."

"Someone…" I wanted to be sure I knew exactly what I knew exactly.

"A man."

"Who? I'll kill him."

"I won't tell you. You don't know him."

"I'll cut his nuts off."

"You'll do nothing of the sort."

The espresso machine hissed, we talked below the conversation, and raindrops trickled down the front window.

"Do you want a…" My question was cut off by the waitress placing a cup of coffee in front of me.

"Let me know if you two would like anything else," the waitress said, turning to walk away—skilled at knowing when to leave a conversation at a table.

"No," Vicky said emphatically, having anticipated what I was going to ask if I had finished the question. "I want to keep the baby."

"Why?" I asked, but suddenly felt selfish and uncaring.

"I studied enough family dysfunction to know that is not the answer. Not for me at least."

That second part hit me hard. If the child had been mine, I would never have even brought it up.

"How do you know it's not mine?" I asked.

"The timing," she answered. "You were too drunk during that time for it to be yours. You weren't interested in doing what needed to be done to make it happen."

More pain stung through me with sharp guilt slicing away my initial reaction.

"My girlfriend is carrying another man's baby."

"That's the deal. You can leave me. I'd understand."

I shook my head in disbelief.

I looked around us; college students were reading notebooks, retirees were talking politics, and men were scanning newspapers. Everything was normal. And buried in that cafe scene, I felt normal. For the first time in a long time, I was faced with a choice. Keep medicating away my issues or finally face a decision that had nothing to do with me, my alcoholism, or my medical treatment.

"No," I said, catching myself smiling, and letting it warm me with genuine emotion. "Who'd raise the kid? He needs a father.

Someone to show him how to hit a baseball. Or, if it's a girl, I will show her how to do ballet pirouettes."

Vicky actually laughed at the vision of *that*. It was a sincere laugh that wrapped itself around me. She nodded, and wiped her eyes again.

"Mike, you should have seen the farm today as the sun rose. The fields turned emerald, the trees ignited green, and the buildings lit up red, as the sunlight slanted onto the farmyard and pried its way onto the valley. There were no words for its beauty."

"It's a sign," I said. "This whole day is a sign."

"You don't need to stay with me. We'll be alright at the farm."

"You need help raising a child. A boy without a father is a fucked-up kid."

"We'd manage."

"Children are expensive. I've got my disability pay. We can afford a child. A boy needs a baseball mitt. A girl needs nice clothes. Bassinets, formula, toys. Hell, a house!"

"We'd be a real family," Vicky added.

It was time to stop my mental illness routine. It had defined my life for too long, and now I was to be a father, mentally ill or not. I had leaned on my mental illness as an excuse for all my life's failures. Our child needed a father who stood on his feet, made decisions, ran the household, and loved his or her mother. The head of psychiatry at the VA once told me the greatest gift a man can give his children was to love their mother. I loved Vicky and we were halfway there. I resolved—right then and right there—to be healthy, not nuts.

"Yes," I said. "And you know, I went off to fight someone else's fucking war, and I think I would rather stay and raise some-fucking-one else's baby … if you want me."

"I love you, Mike. Of course I want you," Vicky said, wiping a different set of tears away from her eyes before adding, "and the baby *needs* you."

And as easy as taking two buses to a cafe, we were expecting.

A soon-to-be-father now, I needed sobriety and sanity more than ever, so I admitted myself to the psych ward for 10 days to dry out. I realized the baby needed a sober daddy without the potential irresponsibility of a lush. It took my forthcoming fatherhood to shock me into seeing the depths of my alcoholism. Only the power of the psych ward counteracted the booze that flowed through my system.

I sat in the waiting room right outside the window to the nurse's desk. The surroundings were familiar—they never changed. Government health care at its best. But, with that visit, I was changing. It's hard to explain. My condition was still basically unhealthy, but now I had a new reason to work harder for my health and sobriety. Of course, I was still on antipsychotics, but I wanted the dose reduced.

"Come on back, Mike," a nurse said, suddenly standing in the doorway leading back to the examination rooms and the doctors' offices. After stopping to weigh me in and take my blood pressure, she led me back to an office.

A man in civilian clothes—a new doctor—not wearing the usual white smock, came into the office and, out of nowhere, asked me if I was hearing voices. I thought it was a strange question, but he was relaxed and composed with a soothing voice.

"Yes," I admitted. I knew I should not be hearing voices, but the sound of his voice pulled the honest answer out of me.

"What are they saying?" he asked.

"Different things," I said. I didn't want to tell him they were voices from the same old jungle saying the same old thing—"we got 'em runnin', Sarge! We sure got 'em runnin.'"

"Whose voice, is it?"

"The voice of the man in command of the tent camp where I lived," I lied.

"We'll give you something, so you won't hear the voices," the doctor said.

I got a sudden feeling that he was trying to justify his job by giving me medicine, and the positive outlook I had had in the waiting room dimmed.

I sat catatonically, until a nurse's aide brought in pajamas.

But I was intent on getting well, so for the next 10 days, I followed the doctor's orders. I played volleyball in the fenced-in gym on the roof with orderlies. I went to Occupational Therapy until I overdosed on making leather belts, moccasins, and wallets. I went to the Patients' Lounge, watched TV, and played cribbage with WWII veterans twice my age. I went to the patient library and took out Rudyard Kipling's *Kim*—"friend of the world"— a habit I adopted in my battle with mental illness. I bowled in the alleys of the old hospital—feeling odd in pajamas and bowling shoes—and bought cigarettes in the canteen.

My grandmother once told me health, family, and job were important in that order. I told myself that every chance I could. It became my in-patient mantra.

Vicky came during visiting hours every day. That was the best medicine of all.

* * *

Vicky's contractions were coming quicker as we entered the emergency room. Immediately, as I was answering a set of necessary questions, nurses rushed her onto a table and rolled her to the delivery room. I paced and napped and read a stack of outdated *Field & Stream* for the next twenty-five hours, but then, when an angelic nurse came out with tidings of great joy, it was over.

Emma was in the world.

FAMILY

I resolved—right then and right there—to be healthy, not nuts.

T**HAT WAS EASY TO** think. It was going to take a lot more work to make it happen. But I made some clear resolutions, and that was a start. Seeing Emma at Vicky's breast was my white light experience.

Every thought I had in some way or another revolved around Emma, her chances for a good life, and the upbringing Vicky and I could give her.

"But what can I contribute to Emma besides money?" I asked Vicky as she breastfed Emma and we sat on the loveseat, watching television. "What can I teach her, besides a love of the outdoors?"

"That's plenty."

"How did the saying go? 'Teach a child to work and they eat for one day; teach them to fish and they eat forever.'"

"I don't think that is the way the saying goes, but that is what you know. That is what she will learn. Skiing, hunting, and fishing," Vicky said.

"Emma won't need ballet lessons; she won't be that kind of girl. If she is a tomboy, so be it," I said.

"You can help Emma with her homework. I want her to do well in school."

"We can be presentable when Emma brings her friends to the house. We want a daughter who is proud of her parents."

"How about her boyfriends?" Vicky asked.

"I'd wait at the door with a shotgun if they didn't treat her right."

***

My dearest Mike,

Happy anniversary!

I love you.

There. I said it. You shouldn't question my love for you for as long as we live.

Yes, Emma is another man's baby, but you have taken to her so, as if she was your own, that I could never imagine her without you. She hangs on to your every word, comes to you when we play on the carpet, and loves to be in your arms. She is your daughter as much as mine.

You are Emma's father, despite not contributing any DNA. I want you to know that.

My attraction toward you has not waned. We have been married a year and we do everything together, fishing, hunting, and skiing. I love you in a way that transcends time, the outdoors, and our love for Emma. I love you besides these things, and I hope you love me in the same way.

I learned from the early times of our sobriety the value of a clear mind, and a kiss goodbye as I drive to work. We've learned from our mistakes, and our sobriety has settled to a fact. Yes, Mike, I love you, and look forward to a spring in the turkey blind, summer on Lake Mille Lacs, duck hunting in Anoka, and skiing in Welch Village. We are inseparable.

I'll leave this note for you tonight, so you'll have something to read tomorrow. Sweet dreams.

Love,

Vicky

EMMA

"HERE IT COMES. AN airplane full of smushed-up carrots. Open up the hangar. Zoom! Right in!

"Such a big, good girl eater! Did you have enough? Want some more? Hmmm, how about roast beef?

"What do you think about fish? Your father wants to take you fishing. He thinks you'll like it. He will teach you. Probably the only thing he likes better than reading to you is fishing—or duck hunting. You'll probably have your own shotgun by the time you are five.

"Look at that smile. You'd like a shotgun? Or is it the roast beef? Open wide.

"What do you two do when I am at work? Have adventures? I bet he plays with our toys more than you do.

"Still hungry? Oh, my goodness! Kids in China are starving, and you sit in your high chair and eat us out of house and home! *Good* girl. You keep eating until you are fat and pretty. That's what your grandfather used to tell me. He said I was fat and pretty. I think it was just to keep me eating so the boys wouldn't be attracted to me too soon. But that's good. We don't want boys attracted to you too soon either—so get fat and pretty.

"You're all done? No more airplanes? Here, one more bite. Good girl. Now let's get you out of your chair and down to the floor so Poochie can lick your face clean! No! Let's wipe your face before you get smooches from Poochie. There we go.

"Let me clean up your little mess, and then we can take a walk outside. You better get used to being outside. Your father will make sure that is where you spend most of your time. He loves the outdoors, and since we love him, we love the outdoors, too.

"There you go, sit right there. Here comes Poochie. You two are like brother and sister!

"Okay—that plate can wait—let's go out to the porch and get the stroller. Here we go. There. Look at the leaves. They're turning. Yellow, red, orange, and wine colored. That's right. Go nuts. You're uncontrollable out here. What a strange baby.

"What a strange baby I love so much! My Emma. Mike and Vicky's little girl—sweet Emma."

CABLE

TO CELEBRATE MY TWO years of sobriety, I took Vicky and Emma to northern Wisconsin, where my father and I had fished on the Namekagon River. We drove up I35E to Highway 70 to Highway 63 as I pointed out the sights, the town of Siren struck by a tornado, the Moccasin Bar in Hayward, with the world's biggest muskie in a glass case, and then our destination, Cable, with a cafe, a corner bar, a friendly community, great fishing, and not much else.

Taking a beautiful woman three hours north to meet the people in a fishing village was relaxing and it was good to interact with other people. I had recently been working on a theory—actually an extension of my fatherhood-is-good-for-the-soul theory—that the most powerful medicine, maybe even the oldest, in a mentally ill person's tool kit was socializing.

"See the woods? The forests in Wisconsin are deep blue. In Minnesota they are green," I pointed out.

"I did not notice." Vicky responded.

"We are staying with friends of the family."

"You said they have three bedrooms."

"Yes. Joanne stays in the main bedroom on the first floor."

Emma looked out the window from her bassinet laying in the back seat. I handed her a bottle as Vicky drove confidently along the two-way highway through the woods. Emma rode well, a happy baby and an easy traveler. She laughed a lot, in response to Vicky's laughter at my stories. She would sleep or sit up in the bassinet or sometimes sit in the back seat or stand up and lean over the front seat. She loved being the center of our attention, and we loved her to be the center of our attention. It was a great family foundation.

In Cable, we ran around town from the Green Roof Inn to Lake Woods Resort to the American Legion Club. Then we drove past the sign that marked the way to Four Seasons Restaurant, along the curvy road past the dam, to Joanne's house that stood with one light on, along the shore of Lake Namakagon. We took it slow because of deer and bears on the road.

That night, as a direct result of Joanne's hospitality and having had a long day, we slept well. The nearest neighbor was across the lake while the nearest city of any size was Duluth—73 miles away across Lake Superior.

In the morning, Joanne made oatmeal, and we looked out at the lake that sparkled in the sun with little whitecaps dancing downwind. Vicky took Emma for a walk while Joanne and I caught up on the affairs of the town.

Vicky returned flush with excitement with Emma in her arms, and said, "It's so beautiful up here! We saw a deer and fawn leap across the road!"

"They better watch out for hunters," Joanne said, unimpressed at a scene she saw almost daily.

"The woods are so deep compared to Minnesota," Vicky said.

"Tell Joanne about your job. Vicky works on Wilhelm Dairy Farm," I said.

"I get up at four in the morning, Mike makes me lunch, and I drive half an hour to a farm with one hundred cows. We milk them, which takes three hours, put them to pasture, and let them be cows. Then we milk them again at five in the night. Then I come home to my daughter and my darling husband's cooking."

"Is Mike a good cook?"

"Limited variety, but delicious."

"Are you ready for your trout fishing lesson?" I asked Emma.

"The fishing is not very good on the river," Joanne said. "The lake is where you'll catch them."

"We're going to try the river first anyway."

I brought in two fly rods from the car, assembled them, attached reels, threaded line, inserted leaders, and tied on two flies—bumblebees, because they were easy to see. I latched the black and yellow flies to eyelets on the leaders. Vicky held Emma and watched me do this.

"Doesn't the fly have to match the bugs floating in the river?"

"Yes, but these bumblebees will be better for your first time fly fishing. It's different than fishing from a boat."

Vicky paid attention to my lesson.

And I was excited. Our daughter was going to go fishing with us. Hardly past the mewling stage, Emma rode well in her papoose sling on my back. She reveled in the outdoors and was happier than indoors. Emma was Nature Girl's daughter, love of the outdoors in her chromosomes, she came to life as soon as we shut the house door behind her. She purred, chuckled, and cooed when sunlight hit her face.

We placed the rods down the middle of the car and bounced over the roads to the Namekagon River. After a short drive, there was an area where we could safely pull off the road and enjoy clear access to the river. We got out, grabbed our rods, and walked down the little bank to the river that rushed past us, around rocks, over logs, and under tree branches. The sun flashed off the ripples, and eddies rotated with foam. Vicky put Emma in her papoose carrier on my back, and I stepped into the river.

"Follow me," I said, and we stepped into the current that rushed past our blue jeaned legs. The cold water came as a shock. We struggled to stand upright.

"Oh, that's cold!" Vicky said as she stepped deeper into the stream.

"Watch out for the holes!" I yelled, as she stepped into a hole that took her up to her waist in water. She gasped as the cold water took her breath away.

"*Now* you tell me! If anything happens to Emma, I'll string you up by the balls!"

"She likes this."

Emma laughed, rejoiced, and raised her arms, in praise of the river we navigated.

Up to her waist in rushing water, Vicky struggled to get on higher ground. Determined, she fought her way up, leaning against the powerful stream. Then she was out of the hole, up to her knees in water, smiling, and holding her fly rod. "What are you doing to me?"

"Okay, now? Here's the first lesson. Hold the rod up with your wrist and swing it from ten o'clock to two o'clock."

"Like that?" She was a natural and did it as I said and demonstrated a knack for the motion.

"Keep that up and let out a little line. Not a lot. Just a few feet."

She rolled the rod back and forth, stripped a little line from the reel, and kept the line in the air, moving the rod back and forth.

Emma watched over my shoulder as her mother flyfished.

"Very good. Now lay the line on the water." She did and ten feet of Berkley fly line with a leader and a bumblebee fly drifted downstream.

"Let it go. Watch what it does. See how it curls around that rock? That's where the trout are."

"What do I do now?"

"Nothing. That's your first lesson. Leave the line in the water. That's where the trout are. Not in the air. A lot of people think trout fishing is casting a line. The trout are not in the air. They're in the water, just like you are now."

"Nothing's biting," Vicky said.

Emma laughed at that statement.

"Try another place. With a rolling motion, roll your line out of the water, cast back and forth until you're over where you want to be, and lay the line down again. You're laying the line down, not the fly."

"Like this?" She oscillated the rod toward another rock, let the line go, and the line settled onto the surface of the water that took the fly swirling around a rock that divided the current into rushing halves. The fly drifted toward the rock then dipped under it as the current tore it away. Emma clapped her hands in delight as Vicky took quickly to beginner's fly fishing.

"That's it. Perfect!" I yelled. "Now leave the fly in the water, that's where the fish are, then roll your line out of there for another cast."

"This is fun."

We stood in the middle of the Namekagon River, current rushing around our legs, as it cascaded its way to the St. Croix River fifty miles away.

"You're trout fishing. The man who taught me the fish were in the water, not the air, had me to his house for a venison dinner. It tasted like prime rib. Try a few more casts then, we'll move downriver."

"I like this."

"It's more fun if we're catching fish."

I slipped on a rock and fell in the river. Emma got wet, submerged for a moment, and came up laughing.

"Mike, that terrified me. Make sure she's not choking."

"She's fine, Vicky. Takes more than a baptism to scare Emma."

Vicky tried a few casts then we walked downriver, and I cast, too, showing her how far I could lay out the line.

"Wise ass. I'll never be able to do that."

Emma laid heavily on my back, clear of the movement of my arm and laughed as I laid out the line.

"Sure, you will. Throw it straight ahead of you into the current. Then let the river take the fly where it wants to go."

"I can't get that much line out."

"Sure, you can."

She moved the rod back and forth, let out the line, and laid her fly twenty yards downriver.

"That's better. Now leave your line in the water. It's called trout fishing, not trout casting."

"You show me."

I moved my rod back and forth, stripped line, cast again, stripped line, kept casting, and let out line, until I had thirty yards leveling over the water, between the overhanging brush, and above the rocks, logs, and barreling current of the Namekagon River. Then I laid the line in the water and let the current take it downstream.

"I'm impressed."

"Nothing to it." I reassured her, glad to be in the river with the calm, soothing patience of the natural scene. There was no place better in the world to be.

"Easy for you to say," Vicky said.

"See how much line you can let out. Impress your daughter."

"Okay."

The current made the river flash in the sunlight and dance around rocks and logs. The river was narrow, not a fly rod's cast to the other side, and curved every forty yards or so. Trees and brush lay close onshore and overhung the rushing water.

Vicky began casting, back and forth, from ten o'clock to two o'clock, letting out line, casting, letting out line, until her line paralleled the water by almost thirty yards. She threw the line like a pro, tossing it out then bringing it back over her head, behind her, and throwing it ahead again. She was in control of the line as it traveled ahead, overhead, behind her, and she cast again.

"Wow! Now lay it down. Just release it. Let the line float down. That's it. Well done. Now, let the current take the fly wherever it wants." The bumblebee swirled in the current, rose, and fell around the rocks then streamed, as the line straightened to its full length. "You did it!"

Emma laughed and clapped her hands, riding easily on my back, looking over my shoulder at the current around my knees. Unafraid, she laughed with the sound of the river gurgling past us, roaring in places, and rushing along, on its way to the St. Croix River, the Mississippi River, and the Gulf of Mexico.

"It's not easy."

"I learned to fly cast when I was thirteen years old. A friend's family had a cabin on a trout stream. His father cooked our fish in butter and almonds on a grill onshore."

"Sounds heavenly."

"It was," I confirmed. "But, come on, it's getting late. Let's wade back upstream to the car. We can change into dry clothes while we wish we had caught some fish."

Emma had fallen asleep on my back, and Vicky was wading through the current ahead of me. For the first time in a long time, I felt welcomed into the landscape of the people and the places I loved.

WELCH VILLAGE

VICKY PULLED UP IN her 1962 Oldsmobile Starfire, with its bald tires, rusted floorboards, and crunched, right front quarter panel from a drunken ride home in a different life. I threw my skis and poles in the car, put my boot bag in the back seat, and gave her directions to Welch Village, one hour south. She wanted to see me ski. Emma lay in my lap, not knowing what to make of the skis and boots lying next to her.

Both sober now, we let no moss grow on our asses. To quote the Big Book, the A.A. Bible, "We A.A.s are active folk." Vicky came up with projects every weekend for us, and often with others. With bars off limits, that left God's creation. And one day at a time, that was alright with us.

Profoundly mentally ill all these years, my body stayed healthy if I did not drink. I skied to excess the entire ski season. My body reveled in the sport, and I walked three miles a day in the off season to stay in shape for skiing. I convinced myself, mental illness did not preclude staying in shape.

Vicky liked sports, but did not have any sport particularly in mind when I asked her favorite. She doubted I skied as well as I claimed, but took an interest in skiing as a test case, to see if I was on the level. She had seen me ski from our days at Jackson Hole, but wanted to get Emma acclimated to the sport. I had become a master skier from all my precious days on the slopes, and Vicky wanted to see me ski at that level. I hadn't been skiing for two years. I, admittedly, was a little nervous about getting back on the slopes, but tried not to show it.

"What does it mean to be a master skier?"

"There are changes, if you want to call them that."

"What?"

"First, I stand straight on my skis. That's new. A professional skier notices it. I'm not leaning back or ahead of my bindings, but right over them. It's difficult to describe. I am perfectly balanced on my skis, left to right, forward and back, throughout my turns all the way to the bottom of the run."

"Okay."

"Second, I have a sense of snow. Eskimos have hundreds of words for snow. I have ten or twenty."

"Like what? Say them."

"Corn snow, powder, mashed potatoes, granular, groomed, boilerplate, ice, Ivory snowflakes, champagne. Those kinds of words."

"How do you become a master skier?"

"You must ski a lot and work on it."

We got on the highway to Hastings, passed the railroad roundhouses, on our way to a bedroom community of St. Paul. I was feeling better psychologically, my emotions fuller, and my thoughts clearer. I breathed deeper, connected the dots in my mind, and my body relaxed to a degree. Life was going better, my psychologist was pleased with my activities, and my positive attitude took over. I was going skiing with a beautiful woman and our daughter, who loved hearing Vicky and me talk. I loved to talk to Vicky, and Emma picked up on this as I told Vicky stories about skiing.

We got south of town, into the farmland, where barbed wire fences protected snow covered fields and crows blackjacked the white expanse. To pass the time, I told Vicky about the evolution of ski equipment. "I got a pair of hickory slats with leather straps for stocking stuffers one Christmas. Took them on a hill behind our house, made one turn, and fell in love with skiing."

"One turn?"

"I became deranged. It was like a tectonic shift in my brain."

"I had one of those. With farm animals. I know what you mean."

"Then my father bought me a real pair of skis, with metal edges, with screws, and painted black. They had spring bindings to keep my leather boots in place. The boots were hardly more than tennis shoes."

"He bought you boots, too?" Vicky asked.

"Yes. Then he bought me a pair of Hart Galaxy IIs, a metal ski too long to ski today, since technology has changed. They were white and weighed a ton."

We turned left onto the highway to Red Wing. "Where is this place? How's Emma?"

"She's fine." Emma's eyes closed and her head lolled to one side. "We have a well-behaved baby. She looks out the window and watches the world go by, or sleeps."

"Is this the turn?"

"Yes. Take a right at that church with the cemetery."

She followed the road that took us into a canyon, past Welch Village, with a bar, post office, and bed and breakfast, then over a little river with a tubing shed. Then we proceeded on a dirt road below a cliff, until we came to a parking lot and the ski area that ascended in a snow field a quarter mile high. I carried my skis to a picnic table in front of the chalet.

I bought a lift ticket then we walked up to the deck to put on my boots, Emma on Vicky's back in her papoose sling. The chalet was crowded with young people in racing bibs and parents, pulling on boots and gloves, drinking coffee, or putting on parkas. The tables were full of gear and there was nowhere to leave my bag. We found a corner, I took out my boots, and shocked, Vicky asked, "What did you pay for those?" They were Nordica boots, red plastic, with silver buckles, and went up to my shins.

"Not that much," I said."

"Yeah, I bet. They're beautiful."

I put them on, using all my strength to get my feet into them.

"They're supposed to fit this way." I clamped the buckles down tight. "Racers clamp them down until they hurt."

"Where'd you get them?"

"Joe's Sporting Goods. Where I get all my equipment. Skis, poles, boots, even these gloves. Put the helmet on. They're just coming in vogue. For safety."

She put on the helmet and laughed. "You can't be serious."

"A lot of protection, right?" I took the helmet off her head, put it on my head, and zipped up my parka. "Come on. You can watch me here or inside."

"I'd rather be outside." We walked down the metal grated steps to the picnic table where I had placed my skis and I put them on, clamping my boots into the bindings. Emma looked over Vicky's shoulder from the papoose.

"I have to get to that chairlift over there," I said, as I put my gloves through the straps of my poles.

"I want to see you do that."

I skated toward the lift, my legs pushing in a scissoring motion, poling, as my belly got a workout. I had not skied in two years, but it was like riding a bike. I waited in line, got on the lift with two other men, and the lift swung us uphill, between the woods and above the snow, dotted with animal tracks.

At the top, I stepped off the chairlift to the right and skated to the top of the hill. I looked below me, saw the Cannon River, the overflow parking lot, and the chalet, in front of which stood Vicky in a blue coat and Emma's face at her shoulder. She waved. I pushed off, steered slowly to get my ski legs, made a snowplow turn, then stem christies to build rhythm, then opened them up, and made long, arcing, driving turns to the bottom, where I swept to a stop in front of Vicky and Emma.

"Show off," she said. "Let's see you do that on that hill over there."

"That's an expert hill. A black diamond."

I skated to the lift, took it to the top, then skated to the left this time. I pushed off, soon was ripping, and made my first turn, driving my knees into it, then the next turn and the next, wedeling down the pitch that fell away from my skis as they hammered the surface of the groomed snow. I kept up the rhythm, driving my knees into each turn, blocking my outside hip, in the French technique I learned at the age of sixteen in Montana. I garlanded down the hill, turn after turn, driving, leaning forward, into my boots, to the bottom, where Vicky applauded. Emma laughed and reached for me with her pudgy hands.

"How's that?" I asked, taking Emma in my arms.

"You are a show off," Vicky smiled. So, buy us lunch. It's your payment for me driving you down here." She walked in the snow toward the chalet, and I pushed my skis alongside her. I bought her a lunch of wild rice soup.

I skied a little more, Vicky watched from the picnic table, then I took off my skis and boots, and carried them to her car. Vicky carried Emma through the muddy parking lot.

"I have a confession," I said.

"Go ahead."

"My illness is going away."

"How can you tell?"

"I'm beginning to make sense when I talk. I have a glimmer of good cheer for my fellow human beings. The agony I've lived in is lessening, I don't know if I'll ever be myself again, but I'm starting to accept my lot in life. I don't dwell on being in the Army. You know, all that happened."

"You're going to make it." Vicky said, taking my hand as we walked.

BUFFALO LAKE

MY DOCTORS WANTED ME to stay engaged in life. Only a few times during the course of my illness did I shrink in the face of responsibility or experience. I leapt from lake to lake, field to field, and river to river, to engorge myself on God's earth. I exposed my belly to God's creation. I tried to lead my life—for the most part—like I was not sick and perfectly capable of getting what I wanted. I was sober, which meant life became a moonshot. I had money and time to spend it. All my service-connected wealth went toward gas for my brother's boat, shotgun shells, bait, licenses, Vicky, and, of course, Emma.

At Buffalo Lake, I had spent all day in an ice castle, holding a jig pole over a hole in the ice, fishing for walleye that never bit, and thinking about Vicky. The shack isolated me, its four walls confined me, and the wind howled, as I changed minnows, dipped the jig pole up and down. Subject to claustrophobia, I had grown anxious in the confines of the ice castle, and it had potentiated my mental illness, and brought back a sense of fear. My neck and shoulders were tense as I sat and stared into the hole cut in the ice where the water became a mirror. Images surfaced.

"Hey, Sergeant. Catching anything?" Ben Gillette's face was rippling along the top of the water.

I closed my eyes, telling myself to let the image go.

"It won't work. You can't wish me away," Ben persisted. I opened my eyes, and saw him—a watery vision of Ben Gillette. I clenched my teeth and didn't reply.

"Come on," he said, "I know you. You can't fake being healthy to me."

"You're dead," I finally said.

"Hell, Sergeant, we're all dead. Every soldier who went to Vietnam is dead—even the ones who made it back. *Fucking* dead."

He cussed with venom. A green bamboo viper crawled over his shoulder coming out of the water, its tongue flicking, searching for warmth.

"He's dead," the snake said.

"I'm not dead," I argued. "I have never been so alive."

"You were alive in the firefights, liar," Ben Gillette said.

I stared at him; the snake smiled, then slid back into the water.

I shook my head slowly.

"Oh, yes," he said.

I watched him, and his face peeled away from the structure of his bones as blood swirled in the water. I caught myself breathing hard, and his eyes narrowed, staring me into a state of anxiety.

"Doing okay in here," John—the supervisor of the ice fishing event—asked, sticking his head into the ice castle.

His sudden voice startled me, and I must have jumped.

"Hey," he said, "I didn't mean to scare you. You okay?"

Ben Gillete's face was gone, the hole in the ice was just a hole in the ice.

"I'm fine," I said.

"Catching anything?"

I collected my thoughts, turned to look at him, and smiled, "I'm about to."

"Alright, sounds good," he said, leaving.

I stood up and got out of the ice castle, catching my breath. The open air above and around the lake had a therapeutic effect on me. I inhaled deeply, and smiled to myself.

"I am alive, Ben. More so now than ever," I whispered to the sky, the lake, the ice, and the fish I knew I wouldn't even try to catch that day.

RECOVERY

SOBER, I LIVED IN agony, and yearned with all my being to break the shackles that bound me. My psychologist said my breakdown likely would have happened sooner or later, due to a gene in my chromosomes predetermining schizoaffective disorder. I could have been stateside, not in Vietnam, friends and family around me, on a job I liked, or in school, and collapsed anyway. The illness appeared in young adulthood, and a trigger precipitated it.

Vicky held down a job, and the responsibility of milking one hundred cows, twice a day, five days a week, did not lose its glamor for her. Proud of her job, happy with her place in the operation, and liking the people she worked with, made her eager to go to work each day. She took my mental illness as a given, something to allow for, accommodate, and support. Like a lot of people, she thought it was for my lifetime. I prayed too hard and long to accept this viewpoint. I went to my appointments, taking my medication and going to my scheduled appointments at the VA. Serious about my recovery, I sat on the bank of the river in the summer and prayed, watched the barges and boats float by, and admired the wildlife that teemed along the river's shore. I did this for hours and luxuriated in the sun that baked the poison of my illness out of me. I bared my chest to the sunlight, and let its warmth heal me, lifting me heavenward, until satiated with God's creation.

I cherished the warmth in my body, hoarded it, fought for it, and sought it. The warmth came intermittently, and I nurtured it, savoring each moment. I conducted morning devotionals of prayer and meditation, supplemented by sobriety, that brought peace and serenity, as well as plans for each new day.

Then my psychologist asked if I'd like to participate in a study to help me determine people's emotions by the expression on their face. I leapt at the chance, ignoring her warning that the study might not help me but could help others. I told her I had faith the study would help me, too.

So, we started, and I met with two other men and a woman three times a week and watched videos of people talking at the office or home, and their gestures and facial expressions to determine how they felt in each scene. Our psychologist asked us questions about each scenario, we discussed our answers, and improved in reading other people's feelings, by the look on their face or the tone of their voice.

At the same time as the VA study, I engaged in an A.A. Fourth Step workshop. My new sponsor, who wintered, financially independent, in California, had taken me through the first three steps then urged me to find a Fourth Step workshop to get the rest of the steps and back on my feet. I found a workshop that met every Sunday afternoon for seven weeks.

In dyads—talking one on one with complete strangers, walking in the dark behind people carrying candles, and listening to Judy Garland sing "Somewhere over the Rainbow,"—thirty of us participated in the strangest process imaginable. Told to trust the process, we divulged our deepest secrets, played a game where both sides always lost, and made fools of ourselves, humiliated each other, and felt relieved when it ended each Sunday.

We drew up a Fourth-Step worksheet of pros and cons of our character, fears, sex conduct, money habits, and past behavior. In a Fifth Step, we took these sheets to a trusted person and divulged our sins to them, cleansing ourselves, like confession, of personality flaws and things we had done to others. I had picked my minister to hear my Fifth Step.

In the middle of all this, Vicky took me to a speaker meeting at a church in the suburbs. We sat through two speakers, lunch, and a raffle to raise money for the Gopher State Tape Library, a storehouse of A.A. speeches past and present.

Emma attended, too, listening to the speakers from her papoose sling on Vicky's back.

The speaker meeting, made up of a hundred people, many new to A.A. from the looks of them, still guilt ridden, not rejoicing in their sobriety, filled the basement of the church. Two eloquent men regaled us with humor and experience as chemical dependency counselors at Hazelden Treatment Center where they learned forms our alcoholism took. Vicky and I sat with several women, engaging, and glued to what the speakers had to say. When it was over, Vicky, Emma, and I walked to the car, as snowflakes began falling.

We waved goodbye to one of the women with whom we had sat at our table.

I opened the passenger's door, got into Vicky's car, shut the door, and, as easy as a snowflake landing on the windshield, my mental illness went away.

I suspected later this period in my life of intense socialization and self-work catapulted me into a fourth dimension of wellbeing.

But at that moment, I felt it. I knew it.

It lifted as quickly as it had fallen.

SALVATION

I SAT IN MY PSYCHOLOGIST'S office for our monthly meeting. A bookshelf of medical books, diplomas on the wall, two chairs facing her, carpeting, and desk, filled the little room. She rotated in her chair to look at me. She wore black stockings to her knees. She had conducted a study that stabilized me and taught me how to manage my emotions—if not my dreams and moods—in the study that helped cure me. She was extremely good at her job, handled its mumbo jumbo as well as any psychologist who believed in it, and was a gifted problem solver. She supervised the VA's education of post-doctoral candidates in psychology. A kind woman, our relationship went back to when she replaced her predecessor when he retired. She was different with a more liberal, less clinical approach. She didn't want to be called "doctor," she was simply Sasha.

"How do you feel?" she asked.

"I feel wonderful."

"How do you feel about all this, sick one moment and well the next?"

"You call me a survivor, my parents call me a miracle, and Vicky called me healed—she said she saw the difference right away. I breathe deeply, the oxygen going into my lungs meets my peritoneum along the base of my belly."

"You have revolutionized your feelings," Sasha said in a gentle, cajoling voice, sometimes accusatory, sometimes teasing, and always knowing when to criticize and when to praise.

"I have kind thoughts for others, warm feelings for my devotionals each morning, and want to hug humanity, so thrilled I am with myself and my lot in life, proud father to a baby girl and husband to the woman of my dreams."

"You are a lucky man." She handled this turn of events like it was a routine outcome, the way water treated the common cold. She had single-handedly cured a man of an illness thirty years in duration who had been in the psych ward eight times, taking Thorazine for what ailed him.

"I am cured," I said, unabashedly smiling. "It has taken years."

"The cool shade of your house is a relief from the glory of God outside." She smiled, unable to withhold her pleasure at my newfound mental health.

"Cured," I said to Vicky after that appointment. "The word is so foreign to me, not in my lexicon, so beyond my ken, that to apply it to me seems impossible! I was profoundly sick. I have to get used to being cured, get the hang of it, and accept it as a moniker to a man who knew no other way than being sick for so long."

"The illness does not show on your face any more," Vicky remarked.

"Now I am cured and can not think about it as a reality, so accustomed to being sick, it was my default, sick, nuts, a bubble off plumb, one oar in the water, one can short of a six pack, my elevator did not go to the top floor."

"At least you make jokes about it." She did not smile at my jokes. It was still too early for that. She was in the process of relaxing; but not relaxed.

"Ask me how I am doing, and I don't say well, excellent, or chipper, although those are the words to describe me, now that I am out of the abyss, on solid ground. I am fine, not off my rocker."

"You're a happy man," she smiled, opening her arms, inviting me into her loving, genuinely happy embrace.

I felt like I was singing to her.

"That is true. I am happy. That is the first thing you notice about me, not having been happy since the Army, so long ago it was a memory of my youth, not my adulthood."

"We worked our way through it," Vicky stated.

"This happiness feels so … permanent, the smile on my face is not going away, like an idiot, who does not have the brains to worry."

"Or a person who has so much to look forward to." One of her skills was to defuse catastrophes and show them for what they were.

— • • —

"I feel good, for the first time since the day before my breakdown and drench myself in goodwill toward others," I had said to Sasha.

"Do you think you still want to see me?" She had let me make the decision.

"Yes. If I saw you once a month and a psychiatrist every six months for a med check, that would be enough. Can you wean me off the antipsychotics? Do you think I need them?" I wasn't ready to make all the decisions.

"We can start lowering the doses, and keep you on that med check schedule. When do you want to see me again?" she asked, turning to her monthly planner. "Let's keep it to a month. A checkup occasionally won't hurt. You're doing well, now. I have an opening Tuesday, May tenth? That's a month."

"That would be fine."

"See you then."

I thanked her and she walked me to the door to the lobby of the Outpatient Mental Health clinic at the VA. I walked to the cafeteria, bought a Diet Coke, and contemplated God's handiwork. The cafeteria soared four stories to a skylight, with windows of offices and wards on all four sides. Gardens of tropical plants surrounded the dining area, and a young girl tended them, watering each leaf.

I had erased hell out of my mind.

TURKEY HUNTING

VICKY AND I SAT in our lawn chairs in front of the cabin rental and peered over the countryside. Emma was still asleep inside. The day was brightening, the yellow leaves on the ground in the clearing in front of us glowed, and the crows cawed. The woods came alive with the sound of birds, squirrels, geese, and ducks.

"That salesman at Joe's said we were hunting turkeys all wrong."

"What did he say?" Vicky asked.

"He said, we had to sit next to a tree, camouflaged, holding our guns, not moving, for hours. No eating, no coffee, no talking."

"Are turkeys that sensitive?" Both of us looked at the fields in front of us, happy to watch for turkeys, whether they came along or not.

"He said turkeys have a terrific sense of sight and sound. They can't smell anything."

The blind with two windows raised looked onto the field of savannah, and songbirds made their sweet sound in the clearing in front of us.

"It sounds like a cushy way of hunting," Vicky said.

"It does," I agreed, "but the salesman said we had to look for roads where turkeys walked and set up along them."

"I don't know if I can be that still for that long."

Our lawn chairs were comfortable, and we regaled in our luxury.

•—•

We rousted Jeff Hutchinson from bed to guide us to the blind where we would hunt wild turkeys. The storm had roared for most of the night, threatened, sprinkled, slammed, attacked in rocks, then misted, until it dissipated into a dawn.

We followed Jeff in his car to a gravel road past the Rum River, north of Cambridge, to a yellow gate. Jeff parked, opened the gate, flagged us through, then got back in his car, drove around us, and waved for us to follow him into woods of oak trees and white pines that bordered a field of savannah, deep yellow after the pounding rain.

We continued along the road, hardly more than flattened grass that wove around the field and into the woods, then curved to a stop near Blind Six, a pillbox made of creosoted plywood. In front of this sentinel, a clearing within maple and oak trees, littered with leaves, lay wet from the storm. Past the clearing and the surrounding woods, another field of long grass bent to the east from the wind that barreled through.

We stopped, and Jeff took us into the blind before wishing us good hunting and leaving.

● ●

"That bag of Fritos makes noise every time we open it. It crackles." Vicky squeezed the bag to demonstrate.

"We've been talking all morning."

"We scared the turkeys away when we pulled in. They could filter back in, but we make too much noise."

"Do you think that decoy works?" I had placed the rubber, inflatable hen turkey too close to the blind and we could not see it out the window.

"Better than nothing. It's our call that is not working."

"What's wrong with it?"

Vicky made a call on the slate box that didn't sound convincing at all.

"Oh," I said.

"I think Emma could make a better turkey call. We should have brought her."

"She'll be happier with the Hutchinson's. But it does seem weird to leave her with a babysitter."

"Let's bring her next time; no matter what," Vicky said.

"Okay," I said and shifted my attention to the task at hand. "My brother said, make a call when we hear a yelp. Otherwise, stay quiet."

"What does he know about it?" Vicky surveyed the field out the window where she had seen deer and heard geese. The field of savannah glowed yellow outside the dark interior of our blind.

"He shot three turkeys in ten years of hunting."

"That doesn't sound like much," Vicky declared.

"At the rate we are going, three turkeys in ten years sounds like a freezer full of poultry," I said.

Vicky ignored my sarcasm and said, "It's cozy in this blind. I like our lawn chairs."

"I prefer it, too, but we'll never get a turkey hunting this way."

"Let's try the hard way next year. I might like that better than this pillbox. It's mildewed in here."

"We can pick a tree along that grassy road we came in on, hunt together, keep each other warm, and sit together under the camouflaged tarp."

"This would be more fun if we saw a turkey," Vicky said.

"It's nice to get out," I said.

"I wouldn't want to do this alone. It's nice to have someone to talk to."

"I could sit out here all day, especially with you."

"I like having company."

I showed Vicky how to load her shotgun. She called the turkeys, but none replied to cut them off and talk to them to bring one in for a shot. Our decoy stood in the middle of the clearing, so close I could not see it over the windowsill. I watched the ridge between the field and woods surrounding us, on the theory a turkey would strut over to visit us.

The sky darkened, we decided to pull stakes at noon, since we got a late start, and wanted to stay ahead of the storm the weatherman predicted was a doozy. We compared notes on calling, the best position for our fingers on the call, and placed them on the slate for the sweet spot. With the hatches on the windows open, the blind well ventilated, we did not feel claustrophobic.

The yellow leaves on the clearing wet, the bark on the trees black, the effects of the hailstorm Monday showed. The sun had been out when we started hunting, but now clouds socked us in, and the long, yellow grass of the field grew drab in the overcast sky. The woods became dark in gradations, as clouds moved across them.

We wanted to beat the storm home, and I did not want her driving in another hailstorm. She said the wind blew the car around Monday and I thought we hydroplaned. Passing semi-trucks in a thunderstorm in the old car scared me.

It was noon and we packed up, careful not to forget anything. I unloaded Vicky's shotgun, a loaner from my brother, making sure she watched me do it. I wanted her to become familiar with the gun, she would use it again on our turkey hunts, as well as duck or deer hunts down the line.

Vicky and I hunted well together, enjoyed each other's company, and shared an enthusiasm for hunting—even when we didn't bag any game at all.

Back at the cabin, we had to tell the Hutchinsons that we had come up empty. In the past, I would have been so disappointed—like it was a matter of my ego and masculinity to not come back with any game after a hunt—but today, it didn't matter. I had a great day with Vicky, and now it was good to be back at the cabin where Emma brightened our day more than shooting a turkey ever could have.

After we ate, while Emma was occupied with her Fort Apache playset I had bought her at K-Mart, we relaxed in the front yard. Lawn chairs, one red, one blue, with canvas seats held us as we looked across the field where we sat. The woods at the edge of the field were wet from the afternoon storm, and the last rays of the sun sparkled off the water drops. The woods were alive with the sounds of a hundred kinds of birds, and we caught ourselves still listening for a turkey.

"There's no use listening for a turkey now," I laughed.

"If we did, I think I would run after it just to make up for today," Vicky replied.

"It was nice today," I said.

"Yes. It was," Vicky agreed.

We sat in the lawn chairs and looked out on the forest, pitch black, with the sky above the field and swamp darkening with dusk, brightening the light from the cabin extending across the yard. The birds in the woods screeched, chirped, and howled, and an owl hooted next to us as we sat in the chairs, drinking coffee. Vicky held the flashlight as I poured coffee into both cups.

"I wonder what kind of bird makes that sound," I said.

"They've been keeping it up ever since the rain stopped," Vicky replied. "But you're the hunter. What kind of bird is it?"

I smiled. "I really don't know," I said.

"What? The great hunter doesn't know something?"

"I know I love you," I replied, looking at the side of her face in the dying light.

"I love you, too, Mike."

The oaks, maples, and pines soared heavenward, and birds sang like angels. The cabin was rustic and the warm yellow glow from the electric lights inside poured through the windows and onto the clearing like a launching pad to God. Rays of evening sunlight slanted through the trees.

A slight breeze rustled the trees, dark in the still night woods. The woods darkened until the familiar logs, bushes, and branches were dark shadows. The cabin light behind us cast our own shadows out towards the trees. Geese honked a blue streak, ducks quacked, and the birds of the unknown species tweeted.

"It's beautiful, isn't it?" I asked.

Vicky—almost whispering—replied, "Yes."

I looked over her shoulder and saw three deer and a fawn walk between trees past the clearing off to our left. The spots on the fawn were visible in the cabin light, it moved nimbly behind its mother, as the deer passed along the same run deer had used long before any cabin was built here.

"Look," I said in a low voice, getting Vicky to turn around and see the deer. The doe stopped, having heard my voice, and raised her head. The fawn stopped as well, but didn't not notice us. Assessing the danger of our presence, the doe skipped up a step and hurried along the way. The fawn followed. They disappeared into the woods.

The screen door of the cabin slammed shut, and I turned around to see a silhouette of a small girl jumping off the porch.

Emma joined us with a giggling story about some adventure she had experienced that day. I listened and smiled at Vicky.

There was nothing running in the woods, no dangers in the yard, no nightmares, and no visions of snakes or battlefield casualties.

There was only me.

Only Vicky.

Only Emma.

And together we had the outdoors.

ACKNOWLEDGMENTS

Thanks go to many people who risked their careers so I could survive alcoholism and mental illness. Dr. Murtaugh and Dr. Posey of the Minneapolis Veterans Medical Center sent me on week-long vacations hoping I held together.

The Sawyer Country Mental Health Clinic in Wisconsin charged me a pittance for the care of Dr. Irwin and Dr. Mercer.

Thanks go also to my family and friends who put up with me when I was no fun to be with.

Thanks go also to the people at bus stops, and the support of humanity, without whose help I would not have made it.

Thanks also to the staff of Every Third Saturday, the veterans hangout that stuck with me every excruciating word.

Cecilia Kennedy, Editor

Barbara Lockwood, Editor

Kelly Ottiano, Editor

Evangeline Estropia, Product Manager

Pulp Art Studios, Cover Design

Standout Books, Interior Design

Muzammil F., Interior Design

Learn more about us and our stories at
www.runningwildpublishing.com

Loved this story and want more? Follow us at
www.runningwildpublishing.com/rize,
 www.facebook/runningwildpress,
on Twitter @lisadkastner @RunWildBooks

www.ingramcontent.com/pod-product-compliance
Lightning Source LLC
Chambersburg PA
CBHW060345310726
48976CB00003B/723